C000050937

GISELLE LEEB's shor
published in journals, r
including *Best British Sh*
Mslexia, *The Lonely Cr*
Lady Churchill's Rosel
placed and shortlisted in competitions, including
the *Ambit*, *Bridport* and *Mslexia* prizes. She is an
assistant editor at *Reckoning Journal* and a Word
Factory Apprentice Award winner 2019. She grew
up in South Africa and lives in Nottingham.

Web: giselleleeb.com, Twitter: @GiselleKLeeb

GISELLE LEEB

MAMMALS, I THINK WE ARE CALLED

SALT
**MODERN
STORIES**

SALT

CROMER

PUBLISHED BY SALT PUBLISHING 2022

2 4 6 8 10 9 7 5 3

First published in Great Britain in 2022 by
Salt Publishing Ltd
12 Norwich Road, Cromer, Norfolk NR27 0AX United Kingdom

www.saltpublishing.com

Salt Publishing Limited Reg. No. 5293401

A CIP catalogue record for this book is available from the British Library

ISBN 978 1 78463 267 0 (Paperback edition)
ISBN 978 1 78463 268 7 (Electronic edition)

Typeset in Granjon by Salt Publishing

Printed and bound in Great Britain by Clays Ltd, St Ives plc

For Kerrin and Megan. Thank you.

Contents

The Goldfinch Is Fine

ALTHOUGH THE TV station gives the latitude and longitude daily, no one wants to know, except for the weatherman, who takes all of the burden alone. Each time he is forced to recite the giant wave coordinates, he goes home after the report and curls up under the covers and dreams he is floating on top of a swell, its height beyond his comprehension. He wakes crying and reaches for the laptop under his bed. He watches the live stream of the goldfinch, high up in its glacial nest. As long as the goldfinch is OK, it can't happen, he tells himself.

◊

A call from the studio jerks him from an uneasy doze. Can he come in early? Yet another weather special. They might as well call it a 'weather ordinary'. The solitary tree in his narrow back garden is bent halfway to the ground, but when he checks the forecast, it is only an extratropical storm.

He struggles into his new Gore-Tex raincoat. The

opposite of understated, but a hundred percent waterproof. Surprisingly, none of the weather crew has made a joke about it yet, and he's grateful because he's not at all sure that he could laugh. He can no longer wear clothing in colours the shades of deep water. And he has more chance of being seen in yellow.

He squelches through his muddy lawn, battling the wind. The neighbours' children are playing behind their glass patio doors. Too exposed, he thinks. He has met them a few times, exchanging gifts of biscuits or chocolates at Christmas. They used to play in his garden occasionally when they were much younger.

◊

"Slept well?" Kimani, the makeup artist, asks in an arch tone.

The weatherman glances up at him and notices that he also has dark rings under his eyes.

Kimani smears on concealer, then powders the weatherman's face, before adding blusher and a touch of lipstick. "There you go. Ready to weather any storm."

The weatherman struggles to keep his weather face on, serious with a hint of cheer, sweeping his hands across the North-East Atlantic towards the UK in the direction of the low pressure arrows. The enclosed broadcast studio, with its strictly delimited walls and ceiling, no longer calms him. He watches himself on the small screen in front of him, still smiling, still making the occasional joke. It could be worse, he could be a newsreader.

The station has gone full CNN lately: live graphics have

him standing on a gently lapping sea, explaining the increasing frequency of rogue waves, until an animation of a giant wave surges through his body like a materialising ghost.

"Stay warm and dry, folks," he quips, and feels like slapping himself.

Lars, the cameraman, comes over to him after the broadcast, headphones around his neck. The weatherman lifts his chin and tries, unsuccessfully, to relax his facial muscles. Don't scare 'em.

Like his weather reports, the crew's customary bustle has become lacklustre, distracted. Younger than him, they have always treated him with deference, but also as if he is irrelevant. Now they are finally taking a keen interest in the weather, asking questions. What is going to happen, is what they really want to know.

"I just present the weather," has become his stock answer. Which is not entirely true: a qualified meteorologist, he knows both more and less than he would like. But what else can he possibly say?

He couldn't start to explain that 'out there' and 'in here' are phrases he wishes still had currency. At times, his mind reverts to a childish imagining: the studio windows breaking, sharks and God knows what flooding in, hunting. Although, if it does happen, it's unlikely the sea creatures would behave in quite that way.

Lars's last question was about the speed of rogue wave formation, something technical, and he waits for his next with a twinge of dread.

But Lars only asks about the set-up for tomorrow. He towers over the weatherman, but his troubled eyes look so like those of an uncertain child that the weatherman contemplates telling him about the goldfinch to cheer him up.

He dismisses the idea. The goldfinch is his little secret. What would the crew think if they discovered that his private obsession is to watch a small, plain-looking bird nesting high up on a pristine glacier?

He gives Lars an awkward, guilty smile. His carefully cultivated reserved Englishman persona is starting to feel redundant; he's always known that he's far too young for it, and besides, the times are a-changin'.

◊

He bends into the wind on the way home. The worst of the storm has passed, but the grey drizzle he so used to love has transformed into a permanent ominousness.

His garden gate slams itself shut behind him. The neighbours' children stand pressed against the patio doors, their faces distorted through the rivulets streaming down the glass. They wave at him and he waves back. It must be hard for them to be indoors so much.

He lets himself into his house. His home, he used to call it, before he felt that the walls were inadequate. He slaps some cheese slices on white bread and puts them under the grill. He places his laptop on the coffee table and waits for it to boot.

The channel doesn't give the bird's coordinates, but he's worked out a rough set based on the location of the finch on the Quelccaya Ice Cap, high above Cuzco.

The glacier bird is, strictly speaking, a white-winged diuca finch. Not a goldfinch at all, but an ordinary grey and white bird. It is against his training to deliberately mislabel it, but circumstances are hardly usual.

Only one of its kind has ever been captured on camera, nesting on a glacier. Nineteen thousand feet above sea level, its species breeds in an environment with heavy snow, low oxygen, bitter cold, and high winds. Brave! And deserving of gold-feathered status.

He opens the web page and is relieved to see the small bird standing on the edge of a hollow in the ice, its nest of twigs behind it, seemingly immune to the cold.

He has almost forgotten that the finch started off as one of a breeding pair. It seems so long ago now, and everything is moving fast. The chicks flew the nest, only to be found some way down from the summit, sticky lumps dashed against the rocks. Nobody knows what happened to the mother bird. It flew out of the camera frame, never to be seen again.

The camera crew were forced to leave the mountain when the ice began to melt. But the male finch, against its usual patterns, has stayed. It has made its first foray into the unnatural. Or, better, into 'the new natural'. It makes him smile to imagine Lars saying it in his gruff voice, his touch of vulnerability offset by the smell of his robust aftershave. The new natural. Yes, Lars would find that quite funny.

He eats his supper, listening to the finch's high-pitched, melodious notes as daylight brightens the ice around it.

He washes up, then gets out the world map and marks the finch's position, shifting it by less than a degree to compensate for the fact he doesn't know its exact location. He adds his own position, an average of the distance between home and the station.

He uses the coordinates from today's forecast to pencil in the giant wave. Strictly speaking, it is multiple waves. Yet he persists in imagining that there is only one freak wave, reconstituting itself in different locations, a recurring nightmare haunting the North-East Atlantic.

Already, the rogue wave heights have surpassed the estimates of climate models. But the scientists can't agree on how they form, let alone accurately predict where they will appear next.

On impulse, he gets out a red pen and steel ruler and joins their positions with three precise lines. The acute-angled triangle stretches away from him across the vast North Atlantic to the finch in faraway Peru, the volatile wave coordinates tugging at them both from a third point in the middle of the ocean.

He doodles lapping waves around the UK's shores as the rain starts again in earnest, the wind howling. A familiar nervous tension settles into his body: small changes can escalate quickly.

He thinks uneasily about last spring's live weather reports from a ship in the Atlantic. How he'd pretended his grandmother had died to get out of going on the trip. There was no danger, they'd assured him, the waves were calm in spring.

Nobody at the station talks about that crew—

He checks the windows and stuffs towels under the front and back doors. He stares out at the driving rain until it is too dark to see, then goes to bed and watches the goldfinch before he falls into a restless sleep.

◊

He walks to work in the morning, bending himself into the slanting spikes of water. His new raincoat is holding up well. He has added waterproof trousers, an unavoidable dark-blue colour, the only ones in stock.

He wonders if Lars would have gone on that ship. He feels pathetically grateful to be on dry land, until he remembers that London is scarcely above sea level. In the event of flooding, perhaps he could reach the top of The Shard. He imagines being trampled by shoving crowds and discounts the idea. Instead, he slides himself and the goldfinch along the sides of the red triangle, like beads on his childhood abacus, until they have swapped places and he is snug in the nest high up on the glacier while the goldfinch sings to a studio audience, a dark wall of water rising behind it.

Why not tell Lars about the goldfinch? Surely it would cheer him up? But he feels superstitious, as if sharing the goldfinch will somehow hasten its end. He knows this makes no sense. He knows that absolutely anybody can switch on their computer and watch the intimate life of the bird in its nest.

◊

A wonderful calm comes over him as he reports that there have been no new rogue wave coordinates today. Lars hangs about after the broadcast. The weatherman is expecting a question, but Lars takes him firmly by the elbow and steers him towards the cafeteria.

The cafeteria is running short on fresh food. They eat Ginsters Slices, picking at the cold pastry and congealed cheese.

Lars pulls out a hip flask of brandy. "Skol," he says, and they take turns at swigging from it. The weatherman notices that they are not the only ones with alcohol in plain sight.

Lars gazes across the table at him and the weatherman dares a glance into his warm hazel eyes. Lars has a question after all. He wants to know about relative risk. Lars is from Sweden and has to make a difficult decision if he ever wants to go home.

The weatherman thinks it best not to tell him about the Draupner Oil Platform off the coast of Norway. Until a laser-based rangefinder measured an eighty-six foot wave, existing consensus was that such a wave could only happen once every ten thousand years.

He's always liked Lars. He only hopes that his eyes are not transmitting the swelling terror he feels inside. Lars deserves to be comforted. He should tell him about the goldfinch.

Finally, he sighs. "Impossible to be exact," he says.

Lars shrugs. "We may as well finish the flask."

An update comes over the loudspeakers: a storm is approaching, a category one hurricane. They are advised to stay put and to stand by, all night if necessary.

The weatherman excuses himself and goes to the toilets. He sits in a stall and gets out his laptop and watches the goldfinch. It has all come down to this: a small bird in a nest of ice, alone. Unexpectedly, he starts to cry. Why is he still presenting the weather? It is becoming hard to predict anything.

He shuts the laptop and shoves it into his bag.

◊

Bleary with sleep, he struggles to keep up with the arrows.

"Two minutes left," says the director in his earpiece. "And for God's sake, smile."

No graphics today, so he explains how wave height is affected by wind speed and duration.

"Keep dry," he says. "And don't go outside."

In the cafeteria, he slumps over his laptop, too tired to open it. Today's wave coordinates are nowhere near the UK shoreline. And the North-East Atlantic is a large area. But the tallest giant wave ever measured by a buoy occurred just off the Outer Hebrides.

He jerks awake to a banging noise outside, grey light trickling in. The place is deserted. He checks the forecast on his laptop: the hurricane is still out over the ocean.

He puts in his headphones and angles his screen away from the door.

The picture is tilted, the nest half in the frame. He feels a lurch of fear before the bird flutters into view and settles into the nest.

How long will the camera batteries last?

He notices a drip from the top of the ice hollow. He'd forgotten that the glacier is retreating by at least a metre a year.

The viewer numbers are dropping rapidly. Perhaps he will be the last person to see the goldfinch. But the thought makes him nauseous. Before that can happen, he will show the bird to Lars.

◊

The early-morning meteorologist can't get in, so the weatherman stands in front of the green screen, his hands moving numbly.

Three sets of rogue wave coordinates, in three different locations, happening almost simultaneously. He can no longer pretend there is only one wild spirit disturbing the ocean. His red triangle has broken open; it is gathering coordinates, morphing into an unmanageable shape.

Afterwards, Lars invites him outside for a smoke and he agrees, although he gave up years ago. They stand on the roof terrace, sheltering against a wall, constantly relighting their cigarettes.

There had been no questions from the crew this morning. Ironically, he'd noticed them averting their gazes just as he became desperate to make them acknowledge something he no longer wants to bear alone. But irony has become irrelevant.

It feels reckless to stand outside, the strong wind ripping away tension as they watch the sky turning an eerie green. It reminds him of the excitement of his first weather special, reporting on the new hurricanes while hanging onto various balcony railings.

A piece of loose hoarding flies past and they duck reflexively, then look at each other and burst out laughing.

Lars puts an arm around him, and the weatherman dares to lean against him.

He feels exhilarated, like the bird in its nest far above the sea. The new normal. Why had it always seemed so impossible?

It is now certain that Lars will not be going home. All flights grounded and the other option, well . . . The weatherman was aware of Lars watching intently from behind the camera, as he pointed to the small symbols denoting ships that had been in the path of the waves.

He thinks of explaining the conflicting theories of rogue wave formation to Lars. He takes a deep breath, then asks Lars if he'd like to see the bird.

"Why not?" says Lars.

They go down to the cafeteria. There are no catering staff and they help themselves to another Ginsters. The weatherman longs for a strong cup of coffee, but the machine stands dull and quiet. Presenters and crew talk softly or slump across tabletops, the hush occasionally punctured by an anxious phone call in the corridor outside.

"Fire her up," says Lars, and the weatherman opens his laptop and pauses for a second before clicking on the link.

He feels guilty about exposing the bird to yet another gaze, but he is also eager for Lars to see it. He thinks of the chicks and words like crushed, pulverised and dissolved come to mind.

◊

He hadn't thought it necessary to ask Lars to keep it secret.

The first he hears of it is before the lunchtime broadcast. Kimani bends close and whispers confidentially into his ear that the goldfinch footage is not live. That the camera, even if it had any power left, would have collapsed into the melting ice some time ago.

The weatherman feels perturbed. Does Kimani have insider news? How do you know, he wants to ask, but doesn't.

He goes to the cafeteria after the forecast to be alone and watch the goldfinch. It must be live. It must.

Lucy, the researcher, sits down at his table. She smiles knowingly as he half closes his laptop. The goldfinch is a robot, she tells him. "It couldn't survive for so long on its own," she says. "I bet the crew took the real one and released it somewhere safer. I mean, like, how long do birds actually live for, anyway?"

Lars comes over and massages his shoulders, as if they have been going out for years. "Ha! You'll never believe AJ's theory," he says. And he sits down close to him and tells them the story, ignoring his scowl.

The real goldfinch is in a zoo somewhere, with fake ice on a fake Peruvian glacier. The only way it would know is if it hits the edge of the sky circle, built with transparent plastic of course, like in that film with Jim Carrey. What was it called again?

Lucy laughs. Lars squeezes his arm and leaves before he has a chance to respond.

◊

The weatherman is finding it hard to switch on his laptop. He clings to his last image of the goldfinch, the one where the bird flies unnaturally into and out of the nest it should have left long ago if it were obeying nature's laws.

Jorge, the soundman, hovers next to him as the afternoon broadcast is about to start. The goldfinch is not really gold, he claims, in a rare mumbled burst of speech above the muffled music from his headphones. It is spray-painted gold.

He's obviously never seen many real birds. And he definitely hasn't seen the goldfinch. Although, in an odd way, he is closest to the truth.

The weatherman's smile feels too big for his face. "Follow evacuation instructions for coastal areas," he says. "If you are inland, batten down the hatches, folks. On no account go outside."

Lars joins him in the cafeteria after the broadcast. The weatherman narrows his eyes at him.

But Lar's expression is sad. "Sorry about the bird," he says. "I thought it would distract them."

They sit in silence for a moment, listening to the rainbands on the outer edge of the hurricane drum against the windows.

The weatherman reaches across the table and grips Lars's hand. He wants to slip away home while it's still possible, like a naughty boy in a fairy tale, running from a series of dragons. He badly wants Lars to come with him. But he urgently needs to update his map. How can he possibly expose Lars to the burgeoning coordinates that once formed a neat red triangle?

◊

Bent low, torrential rain pounding his body, he can barely push open his gate. He wades through the lake in his front garden and nearly trips over the lone tree, its roots exposed, its branches stretching through the neighbours' smashed patio doors. He glances nervously up at his loosening roof tiles before he finally dashes to his front door, shaking, reprimanding himself for his stupidity in coming home.

He forgot his yellow raincoat and he's soaked. He towels himself down, then starts up his laptop. But the neighbours' children bang at his door. They must have seen him battling up the path. Their parents went out for groceries at the corner shop early this morning, they say. It takes him a moment to realise the import of such a statement, but he decides it's wiser to say nothing.

He fetches more towels, then turns on the TV and takes his laptop into the next room. He pauses before clicking on the link, half expecting to see a golden bird singing victoriously, high above the world.

He sits for a long time, staring at the soggy mush of twigs, at the collapsed edges of the melting ice. Perhaps the bird has flown off the glacier? Perhaps it has just fluttered out of the frame for a moment?

He gets out the map and calculates the coordinates for where it might be. He does not add the words 'if' and 'alive' to the equation.

He crumples up the map. He feels as if he has opened all of the windows and doors to his house and the hurricane is beating in, about to rip off the roof.

Why didn't he invite Lars back? Why didn't he? He calls him again and again, listening repeatedly to the warm tones on his voicemail.

The children have become quite voluble. The eldest, about thirteen, talks incessantly about storms, rain, the parents' trajectory, where he last saw them on his app before the signal died. He gets up frequently and peers out the storm windows.

The weatherman thinks it best to draw the curtains to stop the boy staring plaintively in the direction of his old home. And to stop himself watching the garden gate, hoping that Lars will drop by.

The wind shrieks harder and the electricity goes.

He lights candles. He realises that the children are hungry and heats up tinned spaghetti on the portable stove. He watches them as they eat, sitting in a row on the sofa. Absurdly, it reminds him of campfires. But what sort of ghost stories could he possibly tell?

He thinks of himself, the goldfinch, and the wave, their connecting red lines untethered from his neatly drawn triangle. At any given moment, they could be flung apart, or smashed together.

The youngest starts to cry. The weatherman dutifully pats his head and is surprised at how natural it feels. He wonders if he should have been a parent.

He tries not to go over to the window, to conjure up the figure of Lars opening the gate, struggling up the path, to fall exhausted, but happy, into his arms.

At last, the children sleep and he opens the curtains. The wind has reached hurricane proportions, the garden gate flashing white as it swings violently back and forth.

A sailor described the wave as a wall of water that came out of the darkness like the White Cliffs of Dover, a monster so unimaginable that at first he mistook its foamy crest for clouds on the horizon.

He blinks back his tears and thinks of the goldfinch singing joyfully, he hopes, and live, from a particular time and place that may not, already, be the time and place it was a moment ago.

He thinks of the goldfinch disappearing into a dying swirl of melting ice and electricity.

And it is just then that he sees a gold shape bobbing up the path.

He rushes to the front door and shoulders it open.

Lars holds the raincoat over his head, the dark pressing in behind him. "You might need this," he says, grinning.

Mammals, I Think
We Are Called

I HAVE BEEN sitting at this table forever, staring through the front window at the hare, its eyes two holes in the mask of its face: concentrated circles, deep wishes crowding behind them. The twilight perseveres, a pale blue coating. All I can do is shift my gaze towards the crest of the hill, but it feels as if it too is staring back – small animals live in those rocks, small animals arranged in neat compartments in a box, waiting for a breath of words to wake them up. That's what the writing tutor said.

There were twelve of us sitting round the big table that first afternoon. It seems smaller now, filled as it is with imaginary fur and fuzz, hide and scales.

"To write well, you must loose yourself from your moorings, forget who you are," said the tutor.

Cliché! I rolled my eyes and looked out at the lawn, already feeling oppressed.

The hare sat outside, its silhouette distorted, massive against the endless blue.

The tutor saw it too. "Hares, animals, let's use them," he said.

It seemed a safe enough writing topic; thank God, he wasn't about to launch into metaphysics. Now I wish so much that he'd suggested something else: newspaper headlines, weather, even my parents. Anything else.

The tutor told us he'd found a box on the hill. He'd opened the lid and it was full of miniature, squashed animals – a lion, a bee, a mandrill, lizards. Some were dead.

"You must feed the animals," he said, as we began to write. "Add detail! Make them come alive. The animals are starving." He walked round the table and waved his hand in front of our eyes, as if checking our aliveness. "The animals. Feed them! Help them to grow."

How pretentious, I thought. I raised my eyebrows at Ben, the only one I'd had a chance to chat to so far. He pulled a face and I tried not to laugh. Whatever the tutor's methods, he could write.

In the evening, the tutor arranged us round the fire. He explained that he preferred to hold half the workshops after dinner, in the long light, as he called it. It only got dark after eleven this far north and he wanted us to take advantage of the atmosphere.

Animal Tales, that's what the tutor said the evening's topic was, as he leant a stack of large white cards, neatly trimmed, on the mantelpiece. The topic had seemed spontaneous earlier, but he'd obviously planned it all along. He stood in front of the fire, half grinning, flashing the bee, the lion, the mandrill, each with a neat title, like that Bob Dylan video where he discards the lyrics once he's sung them. Where do the words go after, I thought. I imagined them swirling out into the blue night towards the animals who lived in their box on the hill.

He paced back and forth, pointing at us. "Frog, bat, lion, cat," he barked, throwing the cards into our laps.

It was embarrassing. When he added grunts and paw movements, a sort of bestial charades, it became excruciating. We watched, mute animals waiting for a command, our black eyes reflecting the fire.

"Mandrill," he shouted at me. "Write!"

I pictured the hare staring silently at me through the window. The hare was missing from his stupid cards. Damn his mandrill! I wanted to be the hare. I ended up writing two short pieces and hiding one.

"Read!" he said, picking on me first.

The Mandrill

The mandrill crept into the village at night. The mandrill was clever, a clever, clever monkey. The villagers wanted to kill it, of course. It broke into buildings: stores of grain, electrical outlets, the pub, where it pulled itself a pint, its enormous teeth sticking out of one side of its lopsided grin. It helped itself to goods, it enjoyed itself in the moment. It defecated on a flatscreen TV and left its pint glass on top of a digital radio in for repair. Then it flew into the night on its disgraceful way, a stolen balaclava hiding its bright features from the pursuing police as it belted under a street lamp. On the edge of the village, it let out a high-pitched screech. Then it loped across the golf course and into the forest, deliberately pointing its blue bum in the direction of the villagers.

The tutor said nothing. He looked out of the window, as if searching for something better.

I glanced down at my lap. "I've got another," I said, in a ridiculously small voice.

He just stared at me, so I read.

The Hare

The hare is different to the other animals. It dares to know itself, it goes deeper. It revels in the feel of its coat of fur, its sense of smell, its leaping, its hareness. It watches us from the darkness outside the window. It looks at us through its big, liquid eyes. It is, above all, weary, as if it has waited a long time for something it can't quite get to.

"Did you know that Scottish hares fight each other?" said Ben.

"Box," said the tutor. "The females box the males. To weed out inferior mates." He looked bored. "You," he shouted at Emily, the quiet young woman sitting next to me.

Please don't make me, Emily may as well have been pleading as she started to read in her soft voice.

The Cat

The poor cat was in terrible trouble. She couldn't pay her bills. She wanted to stop. She did. But she couldn't!

Her mother took the saucer of white powder away. "Tough love," she said. But it didn't help at all. "I'm sending you to stay in the countryside for a while," she said.

"For God's sake, add more drama! Throw the cat into the loch. In a sack. With a rock," said the tutor, practically screaming.

Emily started to cry.

The tutor ignored her. "More hare!" he said.

I looked up at him as I read, daring him to say something.

The Hare

The hare's eyes have such depths that you could sink a stone and you would not hear it reach the bottom. The hare would like to be bigger, it would like to be very big. Even though it is bigger than rabbits, it is still too small. For the hare, life is much like it was for people who lived in caves before they discovered weapons: the hare has no choice but to avoid, the hare has no hands. For now, it stares through the window at the humans. The sun is almost gone and its shadow lies long across the lawn. At least, it thinks, looking at the row of pretend animals seated at the long table, at least there are no guns.

"Cook me, eat me, I'm only small," said the tutor, laughing at me, mocking me.

Bastard.

Ben spluttered, and then everybody laughed.

I supposed it was just about possible that the tutor had meant it as a joke. And even if it was at my expense, at least it broke the tension.

"Anybody else to read?" said the tutor, staring out of the window again.

Everyone's heads stayed down.

"Drink, anyone?" asked Ben.

Thankfully, the tutor went to sit at the table, staring silently through the window. We stayed in front of the fire, glugging wine and chatting about where we lived, how long we'd been writing for, that sort of thing.

Needless to say, we ignored the tutor. Eventually, his head sank onto his arms and his eyes closed. He let out a little snore now and then. He's a flake, a phony, I thought, not scary at all.

The tutor sat up, startled, and looked out of the window again.

There was nothing there.

Nice try. It was obvious to me that he had not been asleep. Watching us through the skin of his eyes, I thought, from behind his animal teeth.

He went to bed shortly after, grunting in our direction, his footsteps going reassuringly upstairs.

Ben laughed. "Weird old sod," he said, though the tutor was a lot younger than him, and he refilled our glasses.

I smiled in relief at Emily and she smiled shyly back.

"Oh, I know, let's be the animals on the hill," said Ben.

We went round the circle, grunting and squeaking, getting up and imitating the tutor's animal charades. We did Hitler as a bat – we agreed the tutor was the bat – and the bee pretended to fly out the window and upstairs to sting him. The bee farted and we collapsed. Our laughter was interrupted by a scraping noise from upstairs.

"Bloody hell," slurred Ben, and we crept exaggeratedly to bed, still giggling, in case he came back down.

I was grateful that I'd been assigned to the cottage

outside the main house. I held onto Emily's arm as we stumbled along the path.

"Only two more days," she said. She sighed and looked up at the stars as if in silent prayer.

The next morning, breakfast was a quiet affair. Being hungover didn't help. Even the tutor seemed subdued. This worried me more than if he'd been his usual animal self; I suspected him of plotting some odd exercise for later. I noticed how thin he was, ribs stretching through his T-shirt. I could easily overpower him if we had to fight. Don't be stupid, I told myself.

The tutor was a little on the boring side in his choice of morning exercises. From the savage bear to the gentle deer, I thought. But I sat and brooded, waiting for him to start flapping or crowing or hooting. His hair was thick and dark, his hazel eyes flecked with yellow, his lips plump and girlish. Almost handsome. But his cheekbones seemed too sharply angled for his lush features. Still, good-looking enough, if he'd acted more sanely.

I waited anxiously for fur and feathers to fly, but all he said at the end of the session was, "More writing, this evening."

After lunch, Ben suggested that we walk to the hill. We felt obliged to invite the tutor, but he frowned and declined, saying he had to prepare for the workshop. Perhaps he regretted the night before. We all rushed for our coats.

When we got to the crest of the hill, we searched, half-jokingly, among the rocks. There was, of course, no box of animals or any sign of the earth having been dug up – the grass was long and smooth. We sniggered, making pretend grunts and flicks of the tail. And yet we still did not talk overtly about the tutor. So much easier to think he had just been having a bad day.

"I fart like a bee," said Ben, making a buzzing noise, and we pissed ourselves laughing like schoolkids.

As we neared the house, I ran ahead and hid behind a tree, then lumbered out, screeching, pretending to be the tutor's mandrill. We were rolling about when we noticed the tutor standing at the back door, watching us.

He was wearing a cap. "Hello," he hollered into our sudden silence, like a local farmer meeting us for the first time. "Nice weather we're having."

We began drinking in the late afternoon and continued through dinner. The tutor drank and chatted with us, and it felt as if the night before hadn't happened at all. He was almost friendly as we moved to the fire, still sipping wine. After a few glasses, he slumped down in his chair, beaming at us like a contented farmer with his dogs.

To be fair, the tutor didn't start it, he didn't mention animals at all. The topic was Early Experiences, but it may as well have been Animal Tales: Part Two. The tutor sat quietly. "Can you read first please, Ben," he said.

The Lion

The lion roared from his metal cage in the shopping centre. He had been engaged to perform to the Saturday morning crowds. In '94 such things were still legal, just about. He refused to call it 'the mall'. No Americanization for him! What difference did it make? Only one animal wins in the end: man.

"Make it escape, make it eat something, fuck something,"

said the tutor, his cheeks reddening as his mouth twisted in disgust.

Ben glared at him, but he took no notice.

Round the table we went – fur, scales, bristles and teeth.

The bee buzzed furiously. It too was unsettled, angry that death was the price of its sting. Someone had swiped it and it stung their palm, a tragic consequence of its uncontrolled anger. Now it was going to die. "Why the fuck wasn't I born a wasp?" it cried.

"Make it beg," shrieked the tutor, with an odd leer. "Make it do something an ordinary bee would not."

It was shy Emily, voice trembling, who brought up the hare.

The Cat

The cat sat outside with the hare. She licked the last of the powder off her paws. She longed to be inside the house, drinking with the humans. The cat had no memory. Not even for chasing hares.

The hare knew this. Besides, he was much bigger than this particular cat. The hare sniggered.

Jesus, I thought, can't we have just one peaceful bloody animal?

The tutor didn't even look at Emily. He turned to me, as if he knew I'd write about the hare, as if he'd been saving it for last, a treat. "You read," he said, in a suspiciously soft voice.

By this time, Emily was weeping quietly and I felt it was my duty to take the mood up a notch or two. I pretended to read, making up a few happy sentences as I went along.

The Hare
For now it is enough to feel the blue and long twilight brush upon its back. That is all it needs for now. Funny, who knew peace was so easy.

The tutor's face bunched into a sneer of disbelief. "You know the hare's not like that," he said, and I felt a stab of genuine fear.

Fuck that! I read out what I'd actually written. I couldn't help myself.

The Hare
The hare has gleaming dark eyes that suck you in, shiny pools with bottomless depths. It has strong back legs and it is silent, except for its odd little scream when it ruts. It is big, sometimes huge. The hare is an animal, a mammal. Its life seems random, but it likes to choreograph things: it has its little patch, its habits, it does not hop spontaneously. It is not happy with its lot and it is angry with people, with their fur coats and capes. The hare has no hands and this restricts it; it cannot fight back. The hare would like to know a lot of things, the things that hands and travel would allow.

I swallowed a large mouthful of wine and stared at the deliberately impassive faces of the group, animals sending me back my own reflection.

"Breeding like rabbits! The rabbits will take over the world," said Ben.

"Hares," I said.

"Not much difference," he said, laughing.

"Let's play Hunt the Hare!" said the tutor.

Panic flashed across our faces.

"Don't worry, we'll just pretend," he said.

It was Ben who persuaded us. "Come on, it'll be a laugh," he said. "Anyway, a hare can outrun any of you."

Anything was better than sitting with the tutor.

We held ridiculous torches in our hands, kindling from the fireplace, and we went into the night to flush out the hare, Ben and the tutor small silhouettes ahead of us. I remembered how big the hare had looked in the twilight. I remembered I'd wanted to be the hare.

It would escape.

I almost threw my stick into the bushes – it was a silly game. Silly, silly, I chanted in my head. And embarrassing! I was glad it was too dark to see the others' expressions.

"Look! Look!" someone screamed.

A fully-grown lion raced past us, chasing the hare across the lawn.

I wouldn't have believed it, except that after we got inside and bolted the door, we ran to the window, and there it was, distinct against the navy-blue sky, the hare watching it from some distance away on the path to the hill.

The lion moved closer to the glass and stared in at us, threw back its head and roared – whether in pain or rage, I couldn't tell – and then sped off after the hare.

I hardly remember how I got to bed that night. In my dreams, the bee, the lion, and the cat joined a long line of animals filing from the lawn, back towards their little box on the hill, until the twilight finally lifted and the front window filled with bright sun.

◊

The morning workshop passes mostly in silence, no mention of the night before. The tutor tells us to write a bio. Nobody has to read.

The tutor breaks the silence at the very end. He lifts up his head and says, "I used to have wings. I used to feed berries to squirrels."

Nobody even glances up.

"Only joking. Just getting you in the mood for this evening's session," he says, deadpan.

The silence continues at dinner. I'd vowed not to drink, but I need two thirds of a bottle just to get through the meal.

As soon as we sit down in front of the fire, the tutor says, "Over to you, hare," and he gives me a challenging, strangely jealous look.

I take a slug and meet his gaze.

The Hare
My eyes will engulf you. My teeth, yes, my teeth eat grass, but my eyes make up for it. You think I am scared sitting out here. And it's true I have no hands. Sure, if I knew you had a gun. But you don't, and I'm far too fast for your knife.

"Yeah, right, as if you could outrun me," says the tutor, smiling as if he knows something we don't.

I feel so angry, so openly hostile, I can't look at him. "All I have to do is run," I continue, "run to the very top of that far hill, then sit and watch you approaching up the steep path. And when you are very near, when you cannot help yourself and you look up, then I will turn my eyes on you, then you will see me. My eyes will be enormous. They will suck you in."

I finally look at the tutor. He is staring out the window, his expression inscrutable.

The hare's eyes stare back at him, as if burning through from behind their mask of skin: concentrated circles, their secrets crowding behind, their deepest wishes.

The tutor stares at the hare for a long time. Then he loses it and runs outside onto the lawn.

This can't be real, a trick of the light. Except the tutor is out on the lawn, boxing the hare with his bare hands.

We line up at the window. We stand silent. All words have been wrung from us. Somehow, the hare is as big as the tutor. It has strong back legs. It is kicking him towards the hill, towards oblivion.

We stand, pleased and guilty, until it gets so dark that we can't see a thing.

But in the end, it's not real. The tutor comes in through the back door. "First, catch your hare," he says merrily, holding up a normal-sized, dead hare by its ears.

For a moment, I feel pure hate towards him.

He tells us he killed it before we got here, three days ago, and hung it up in the shed to drain its blood. We don't quite believe him.

The tutor is in the kitchen all of the next morning. "A fur dinner, a flesh dinner," he sings as he joints the hare, prepares the enormous jug. His uncharacteristic heartiness is more unsettling than his bizarre moods and I look forward to leaving after an early lunch.

When he brings the hare through, I avoid his gaze. But I sit down in my place. To some, I'm sure it must smell delicious.

"The body of dear small hare," says the tutor, dishing up. He places a steaming plate in front of each of us.

We watch in silence, our food untouched, as he slowly lifts the spoon, chews and savours the mouthful of dark meat for what feels like forever. I realise his relaxed contentment is that of a victor.

But a tear runs down the tutor's face as he puts down his fork.

Hypocrite.

"Let us pray," he says. He bows his head, then intones, without a hint of his usual sarcasm, "Take, eat: this is my body, which is broken for you: this do in remembrance of me." He kneads the edge of the table for a long time, as if only now discovering the joy of hands.

When he finally lifts his head, his expression is elated, like someone whose wishes have all come true.

The tough meat sticks in my mouth like a betrayal.

The tutor talks enthusiastically throughout the meal, his speech odd, halting, phrases articulate but roughly joined together.

I stare at the tutor and he stares back. To my surprise, his eyes have become concentrated circles, big and liquid. A hare's eyes.

He smiles. I feel a genuine warmth between us, and I know he is a completely new creature.

He points at himself, then at me. "Mammals, I think we are called," he says in wonder, enunciating each word as if it is a jewel plucked from a rich store of newly discovered speech.

I smile back. "Yes. Yes!" I say.

I still dream of the long line of animals. I am sitting at the table and they stop, one by one, and gaze at me through the front window, their eyes deep holes, wishing for something more, before they turn and file back to the hill.

Everybody Knows That Place

E VERYBODY KNOWS THAT place. A place that blooms with fresh holidaymakers, excited screaming children, and the recently retired in spanking new motor homes, already too big for their needs – we should have taken our time to choose. The huge family-sized tents. The place where everything is neat and mapped out and simple, where the rituals continue, only slightly transformed: the extra walk to wash the dishes, to take a shower.

The road from the gates leading down to reception, the lawn in front of it neatly edged with a strimmer, the toilets and the recycling bins next to it. The road continuing past reception, then curving sharply left into a straight stretch, the spaces for camper vans demarcated in tarmac to left and right, well-grown, established hedges separating them on each side, electric hook-ups at the ready for plugging in conveniences – fridges, cookers. The hardier campers, with the small tents, relegated to the sloping land in front of the rec room tucked neatly between the pitches, halfway along the right-hand side of the road.

◊

Everybody knew that place, the rec room painted pale green with an injection of funding, the ping-pong table, clean, smooth surface dissected by a net, only slightly ripped. The door standing open, the cracks radiating out from the centre of the window next to it, the fire extinguisher lying on its side in the grass after being used, unsuccessfully, to stave in the hard glass.

The way the place lives on without people, as if waiting for a rescue, a revival. Its reasonably new tarmac not yet vulnerable to the trees' roots. To dereliction. The guest cottages opposite reception, pleasant low white buildings, a good-sized garden in front of each, vandalised, waiting for a potential property developer, protected by warning signs and occasional visits by the police. The grass and soil, recently scraped from the tarmac in a thick mat, the first tentative step to restored health and vigour, already creeping back over the edges – just testing.

◊

This is how it starts, the tour. They don't understand. They don't know they've been there before. They think it's the first time, and once it starts there's something in their bones – what's left of them – that wants to go back in time, to be one of those people in camping trousers, waterproof and shiny with numerous and adequate pockets, who drives the caravan onto the pitch, backs it up again and again to get it level. Who forgot the levelling ramps?

They want to be one of those people, but they can't be. The world has changed, it is too late. They've collectively crossed the threshold, like the grasses growing over the verge where they shouldn't.

And yet they feel it, that tiny tug, like a current, but not quite; it's beyond words and this disturbs them. They know logically that chemical or digital, it's all the same, but nonetheless they can feel it in the parts that are still human, they can feel a hint, a dark wet organic taste, a nostalgia for something they've never actually had.

◊

At the entrance, he waits next to the big sign with the ancient photoshopped picture blending guest houses, motorhomes and tents. "Caravan and Camping Park," it says. The national park opposite has been restored for maximum authenticity. Just don't look too closely at the birds.

He finds himself listlessly plugging and unplugging his left eye from its socket. He's started to wonder about this habit, and he's also secretly proud of it – a nervous tic, really, something more pure human than cyborg. People remove them deliberately for cleaning, but he does it spontaneously, and this feels good. He tries to stop the 'why' following, to try not to explain it.

He unplugs the eye and points it at himself. He looks pretty much the same as everybody else, and that's OK, that's good, otherwise he might be made to feel inferior.

Nobody does these days. It's unnecessary, distressing even. Everyone gets along: no fear, no war. And emotions remain, though faint, like delicate imprints, a slight tang in an otherwise ordinary cup of tea, or 'cuppa', as he's taken to calling it.

But the new theme park has generated faint hints of excitement in him, a recognition perhaps of the ongoing need to connect with fully human roots. Something unexpected, not factored in. They still don't understand it, but they've finally admitted defeat and created the conditions to meet the need.

◊

Everybody knows that place, the hot sun baking down on thin canvas or thicker insulated caravan walls, the afternoon wearing away, too hot for a walk even, an afternoon where perhaps you might just sit in the shade of an awning and find yourself idly plucking grass, tearing it out by the roots, resenting the fresh band of sweat breaking out on your itchy forehead, squinting into the sun, avoiding the gaze of your neighbours, wishing that the separating hedges were higher, that you'd booked a more secluded spot, until, at last, you swipe away flies for the umpteenth time and allow yourself to lie back on the inflatable mattress and close your eyes, face in the shade, calves in the sun, and drift off to sleep and wake up sunburnt, remembering your dream about somebody from your distant past.

◊

He'd had to rent out the space – ten euros per person per day, including the tent (no car) – like the pure humans used to do. Money is unnecessary now that everybody is comfortable. But buying and selling was an important part of the camping experience.

You can only enter the park alone, it says on the ticket, and only one person is allowed per night. There's a long wait, they told him, and the waiting is also new, also part of the experience. The wait is long, but nowhere near as long as it could be. Not everybody is interested in finding their roots. The gap with the pure humans has widened; they are almost at an evolutionary fork and some would prefer to forget: to them, the pure humans are distasteful, like Neanderthals were to pure humans. What's the point, they say. The past isn't going anywhere, and you can always look it up later.

It's all real, it also says on the ticket, and he believes them because they don't lie anymore. There is no reason to lie. But he can't help thinking their grasp of archaic English is not as good as his and they must have meant 'realistic'.

So he finally plugs in his eye and strolls past the sign and through the gate. There are no camper vans or cars parked in front of the reception, and when he pushes open the door to the office, he sees that its dark-green metal is starting to rust and the room beyond is full of smashed furniture and sprayed with graffiti.

He didn't realise that there would be no people, that the park would be derelict. Vandalised. His uneasiness is accompanied by a strange thrill. Nothing is vandalised these days. It makes no sense, and the strong feelings that made the pure humans smash things are sealed up or gone.

Perhaps the experience is starting to work. They'd given him no enhancements, no chips or pills, but they could be using something else to influence his brainwaves.

Permission granted automatically – he hadn't bothered to read the small print on the ticket.

Of course, they said, not all pure humans liked camping, but that only heightened its appeal for those who did. They felt saner and healthier getting back to their roots – a bit like him – which made little sense because, even then, there were no marauding wild tigers or leopards, and they had keys to their motorhomes and could lock themselves in (barring a rare few unfortunates in tents in wildlife parks). And the camper vans had toilets and showers.

But the tent campers were the smuggest, even though they had no chemical toilets and no showers and had to walk – sometimes quite far – in the dark, with their battery-operated headlamps, and sit half-asleep, listening to piped music, and curse because the free toilet paper had run out, and stare at a huge, possibly poisonous spider on the back of a toilet door with a sign that said: Please place feminine hygiene products in the bin provided.

He walks past reception to the white houses and looks into the empty rooms, wires and fittings ripped out – also vandalised. His excitement grows when he sees a hosepipe pumping out precious water.

His shock passes almost too quickly and he instinctively – instinctively! – fills up the complimentary, authentic metal bottle dangling from a karabiner attached to his belt. It can't be real. They would never waste water like that.

It's after five now and the sun is at its hottest. It occurs to him to splash some water on the back of his neck, something he'd seen pure humans do in old films. It feels incredibly good and immediately cooling. He'd forgotten he had a back of neck.

He smiles proudly when he recognises the tap. He struggles to turn it off. Almost too simple a device. He turns it the opposite way and is pleased at his ability to stop the flow.

He looks around, a faint anxiety creeping in. He's been training himself to amplify his emotions – just a little habit, really – but so far he hasn't experienced much anxiety; the circumstances which might cause it rarely occur.

Now he feels odd flutters. He feels as if his eyes are misinterpreting the light. He could adjust them, but that wouldn't be the same somehow. It is sunny and hot, but as he walks past the reception and down the road curving into the stretch with the caravan pitches, the ruined rec room reflecting light from its cracked window, the grass in front of it glowing green, he feels vulnerable.

He's a little thirsty. And hungry. He remembers some of the things the pure humans did to each other, collateral damage to their freedom to feel. Some felt too much and in the wrong way, some too little and in the wrong way. It's a park, he tells himself, no harm can come to you. It's all part of the experience. But in the absence of other campers, the park feels—

It is then that he sees the red tent bag outside the rec room. He stares at it for a moment, wondering who it belongs to, his heartbeat slightly elevated, before he recognises it as his from the picture on the ticket. Next to it is a sleeping bag and a rucksack.

He sips cool water from his metal bottle and feels his heart returning to a steady beat.

He takes the tent from its bag and shakes out two pieces of fabric – the inner, ridiculously flimsy, with an aerated panel, and a camouflage covering, the outer. It has no protective properties, except to keep off the rain, which is far less frequent these days. He forgets his fears and amuses himself with joining the thin poles together. A tiny hiking tent, 2018 model. He knows because it says so on the side – he'd avoided over-researching for once. He clips the inner to the poles. A separated inner and outer to hold off precipitation. Clever, really, in its simple way, and assembled in minutes. Clever, but nonetheless practically useless. Small wonder they had to fence off the parks.

He looks for a place to pitch the tent on the sloping lawn in front of the rec room. The area is open on all sides. The vandals, he thinks, will they return? Or is once enough for them?

He doesn't know.

They are long gone, he finally tells himself, but he leaves the tent and walks further down the road, peering from left to right at the pitches branching off it. The road is long and he thinks that if the vandals did happen to come, it's unlikely they'd go all the way to the end. After all, the police could arrive at any time to interrupt their antisocial acts.

He doesn't know much about vandals' feelings. Nowadays, people are kind and cooperative and mild, because it makes sense to be like that.

Nonetheless, he feels it would not be safe to camp out in the open—

It must be part of the experience, an ancient instinct kicking in, this need to hunt for a secluded spot.

He walks back and forth until he decides to pitch the tent behind one of the dividing hedges near the far end of the road, out of view, in case any vandals pull in for a last smash.

He fetches the naked-looking tent and places it behind the hedge, but he still feels uneasy and decides to move it behind a wall of trees and bushes at the back of the pitch instead.

Once he's completely hidden, he immediately feels better.

The grass is lush and the ground flat and easy to peg. He secures the outer, mismatching the coloured tabs at first – too simple, really, easy to miss. He fetches the sleeping bag and rucksack from the rec area. He spreads out the groundsheet and sits down and looks inside the rucksack: a small mosquito net, insect repellent, a camping stove and pot, a torch, bread, cheese, packets of dehydrated food, salted nuts, and flip-flops.

He is sitting quietly, listening out for vandals, when he realises he can hear birds. Of course, he's heard recordings, but these calls sound real.

They can't be. But he knows that they are. Irrational, but true. True! He feels painful pricks all over his hands and face. Midges. They too seem real. But the sensation reminds him that his skin is sensitive and alive. He remembers this with some wonder.

He sighs, relaxes. He feels authentic, as if he's really there.

He ducks instinctively at a loud roaring noise as the top part of a car flashes past on the road running parallel to the park. A combustion engine! The road is closer than he thought, and the tent is partially exposed to it through a gap in the trees.

The outer is dark green, he reasons. Headlights illuminate forwards. Only a small section of the tent is visible. But what if a passenger is looking in his direction? What if the police arrive and mistake him for a vandal? What if the vandals happen to be driving by and he attracts their attention?

He'd bought a ticket. Of course this isn't real. A few more cars go by; he tells himself they can't see him, though he can't help ducking each time he hears one. He sits for a while, trying to enjoy the sensation of tiny bites on his skin. His uneasiness passes and he laughs to himself at his ridiculous fears.

He hears the low hum of a car driving into the campsite. A car door slams and he jumps. A louder, unidentified slam and he jumps again.

The vandals? Or the police? In either case, he doubts they'll take the trouble to walk all the way down to the end. They wouldn't expect anyone to be here. But what if it is the vandals and they've seen him from the road?

He sits for a long while in rigid silence, starving, too afraid to open the rucksack, let alone try using the stove with its poisonous gas.

At last, the car rumbles away. He realises the second sound was a bin lid slamming down. The police, he decides. Just checking.

But the tension and fear remain, not faint at all, but growing, while, despite his efforts not to think, his rational mind reels away in the background with reasons and explanations and logical possible outcomes that he finds himself whispering out loud.

He begins to itch, to scratch, to forget that he is in a

park. He frantically slaps at the midges, no longer able to appreciate them, his senses overwhelmed by primitive sensations. He puts the mosquito net over his head. He sprays himself with the repugnant-smelling insect repellent and has to sit for a while pinching his nose.

To calm himself, he eats a bright yellow piece of sweaty cheese and a chunk of bread, and then climbs into the tent and tries to sleep, twisting and turning in the hot, tight sleeping bag, his head angled uncomfortably on the rucksack, listening to the cars going by, mentally checking none are turning in.

He doesn't know what time it is when he wakes to the sound of music. Vandals! It is dark and he is well hidden behind his bushes. But what if they saw him from the road? He slides out of his sleeping bag and creeps to the edge of the bushes, suppressing a yell as his hand closes round a spray of thorns and tears of pain prick his eyes.

He peers cautiously round the bushes and stumbles back with fright and surprise. Everything is there: the caravans, the big family tents, the rec room lights blazing in the distance. Although it is dark, it is like the daytime, like what he'd expected to see. This is what it should have been like all along.

The relief almost overpowers him. He can't understand why they have decided to switch it all on in the night, but this hardly matters. And the fear is part of it, he's sure now: a thorough, authentic experience of being human in 2018.

He swallows hard and slowly approaches the camper sitting outside a caravan in a camping chair, not three feet away from him. He can hear twigs cracking as he walks through the bushes, then the slap of his complimentary flip-flops on the tarmac. But the man does not turn around; he reaches into a cooler box and takes out a can of lager. Perhaps he can't hear him above the music from his portable radio?

He had learnt archaic English in preparation. Possible greetings flash through his head: Hello. Hello there. Nice weather. Hot! Well, hello there, nice to meet you. Staying long? A cup of tea?

He feels suddenly unsure of the greeting rituals, although this is one area where he did prepare thoroughly. And surely they'd have programmed the man to know he was coming?

He stands in front of the man and holds out a hand, but the man sips from the can, as if he isn't there.

He gives up and walks past him. Rudeness did happen in campsites. He supposes that friendliness was not obligatory. Rudeness did happen.

Why is he repeating himself?

He had read that sometimes campers do offer a stranger tea so that they have something to talk about when they get home – I met the strangest man. He wishes this friendliness was happening now, like they said it used to, most of the time, anyway.

He stands for a while, wondering whether to approach the campers on the adjacent pitch, looking up at the full moon. It is almost haunting, he thinks. He plays the word over his lips. Haunting. Another new word – and feeling – he'd only read about. Yes, haunting, haunting. The moon is haunting. The whole park is haunting.

He shivers, although it is still warm. It all looks too real.

But it can't be real; pure humans no longer exist. It must be what they used to call 'ghosts'.

His fear overcomes all reasoning. He's sure of it. He's sure. He can't explain why. It is just a feeling. And this is even more frightening, but also exciting.

And then he notices it. A dog. About knee-high, with white and rust patches and a long pink tongue sticking out of its open mouth. He can hardly contain his excitement. A dog! He bends down and holds out a hand. "Here here, doggie doggie."

He takes a deep breath, lets it out slowly. The dog cannot see him. It is also a ghost.

He straightens up, disappointed, but he feels as if something has entered his heart. His heart? He forgets that is not an accurate description. He feels a terrible sadness. The dog so close, but not. He imagines the dog taking a small titbit from his hand in its delicate, sharp teeth. Or even biting him – he almost wants the sensation, like with the thorns, the joy afterwards when the pain subsides.

He studies the man in his camping chair, cracking open another can of lager, and the dog, who, satisfied with an idle pat from the man, wags its long, bushy tail, then lies down in the shade of the man's car.

This is, without a doubt, the most fantastic experience he has ever had. A chair, a beer, a dog. He finally understands the primal simplicity of such a life, itself an echo of something even more ancient. And to think he was worried about the vandals.

A revving noise splits the air. He fights the urge to run for cover. The motorbikes roar towards him, emitting poisonous fumes. The vandals! He can't help running back behind the bushes.

They screech to a halt on the road near the man's pitch. The tension is almost unbearable as they remove their helmets. But the young boys' faces are smiling. If they are vandals, then why do they look so happy? He'd read that vandals were usually unhappy, acting out repressed aggression towards their non-functional parents.

He has got it wrong. The boys park their bikes and nod to the man in the deckchair, who nods back, unperturbed, and leans over to switch the station on his radio to the football scores. The boys are holidaying here, just letting off what they called 'adolescent steam'. They are not vandals. Why would they be when the park is open, even if it's night?

Nevertheless, his heart is thudding in his chest and his mouth is dry. He runs his hand through his hair and wishes he were real, before he remembers that he is real and they are not.

He creeps from behind the bushes and forces himself to walk through the dog and the man to prove there is no danger. They do not notice him and he feels a little better.

He is drawn to the rec room full of shrieking children fighting for their place at the ping-pong table, the ball making a loud noise, back and forth, back and forth. One of them slams the ball into the ceiling and it ricochets off the walls. He covers his ears to block out their raucous laughter.

His fear, his anxiety the pure humans might have called it, has returned. He makes his way slowly back to the tent. Was the ticket spiked?

He crawls into the sleeping bag, wishing the experience was over. He longs for quiet, but the children's shrieks penetrate the thin, synthetic skin of the tent and he can't block them out.

He is woken by the noise of the motorbikes a few hours later. The sleep has done him good. He feels more like himself, and relaxes back onto his not-altogether-uncomfortable, self-inflating, lightweight mat. Nothing to worry about. It is only the hormonal boys. Despite meeting no one, he finally feels like he is fitting in as he pulls up his sleeping bag for the millionth time, rearranges the rucksack pillow, and prepares to sleep on.

But the sound of the engines continues. And now he can hear shouts. He lies still for a while, safe behind his hedge.

He persuades himself to go and look. He is invisible to them, after all. He peeps through the bushes and everything is gone: the man, the dog, the tents, the caravans. The park is back to how it was when he first arrived, derelict and deserted.

Except for the man's camping chair and the cooler box next to it. And the boys on their motorbikes.

His heart threatens to beat out of his chest. This time, there is no mistaking the vandals. His breath held tight, he looks again.

They are shouting to each other, a few of them heading for the rec room on foot. Their smiles are not happy, their bared teeth threatening, the rank smell of testosterone wafting towards him in unpleasant waves as they move with an exaggerated gait.

He is invisible. Invisible! But fear is washing through him.

They are not real. He forces himself to come out from behind the bushes. He ventures onto the road. Nothing can harm him. He can hear the blood rushing in his ears, despite their yells and the noise of the engines. One of them rides round and round in tight circles, spewing poison. Another nearly runs him down as he drives in short, sharp bursts up and down the road.

He makes it to the rec room door unharmed. He is shaking, waves of adrenaline coursing through him, but he stands right next to the boy holding the fire extinguisher and waves his hand in front of his face. The boy definitely can't see him.

He closes the door slowly and deliberately, before the boy can smash in the window, then opens it. That is the first effect he has on their world.

The boy drops the fire extinguisher and backs away, staring, open-mouthed. "Hello?" he says.

And he sees something in the boy's face – fear?

He closes the door again, then shoves it open, slamming it hard against the wall. He goes inside. He picks up a ping-pong bat, the soft padding hardly torn at all. He retrieves the ball from where it has rolled under the table.

He looks back, and now the boy stands frozen in the doorway. He finds another new feeling, one of pleasure at the boy's expression. He stops questioning it. It is just a feeling, after all.

He swings the bat, enjoying the wild sweep of his arm. He throws up the ball, like the children did, and whacks it as hard as he can into the opposite wall so that it ricochets off the ceiling, walls, and floor.

He finds himself laughing loudly as he watches the boy

covering his mouth in horror. The boy can't see him; he can only see the ball.

He runs to fetch the ball. He picks it up, bounces it off the floor, and aims it straight at the boy's face.

The boy screams and ducks.

His laugh sounds odd to him; he has never laughed heartily, and certainly not like this. But he laughs on as the boy streaks away across the grass, ignoring his jeering friends, and jumps onto his motorbike. He laughs as he picks up the fire extinguisher and hurls it through the window, as the other boys run to their motorbikes and speed away.

He feels truly purely human!

He laughs until the park settles around him, the smashed window glass, the fire extinguisher lying freshly abandoned in the grass just beginning to creep over the edges of the tarmac.

He stops laughing and goes to sit in the man's deck-chair. A ghost's chair, he thinks, but it feels real enough. He pretends to enjoy the taste of the beer as he tips it into his mouth in discreetly small sips.

He feels as if he'd like to sit there forever, if only it weren't so lonely.

"Hello," he says. "Hello. Hello. Hello?"

As You Follow

I T IS A bold entrance. You cannot miss it, booming out its
yellow lights and buxom barmaid cartoon, across from
the magnificence of soaring glass. It has beer, beer, beer
and other things besides, if you have the money.

Down the stairs, out of the soft end-of-October rain and
Halloween nearly over. You duck under the low arch, burly
bouncers stopping you, pointing out a far bench, changing their minds, pointing out another, squeezing you in
beside a quiet couple picking at something green, out of
place among the shouting and singing, the plates of leftover
Bratwurst and chips, the men standing and cheering on
the boys in lederhosen, with their brass instruments, their
paid smiles, to keep going and going and the long wooden
trays of spirits, red shots lined up in sixes and twelves, and
on one end a sparkler to set them going, to light the spirits
before dawn, and they go down down down and light up
the insides. And the felt hats all new-looking, hired, and
the voices on and on, louder.

It is ten o'clock and the jackets are thrown over chairs,
over benches, forgotten, and what should hurt the ears is
pure music through this veil of spirits. And the beer steins,

two pints, the biggest glasses you have ever seen in London Town, all the way from Germany.

It is almost the end of Oktoberfest and it is the thirty-first, the barmaids, white aprons streaked with fake blood, pushing through the cobwebs with more flaming trays as a group of men stand and they are going drink, drink, drink, as one of them holds a glass up to his lips and churns his throat, head back.

And next to him you see a child, blue eyes and blond hair, fashionable short back and sides, and he is pointing his young thumbs, beckoning the band closer, suggesting a song and clapping hard as it starts up. And him, him, him, he points. And he is too young to be here, you say to your friend. But the boy is swaggering, confident, he is dressed like the men, in tight-fitting, dark-blue trousers, a pinstriped shirt, and he is happy, happy, he is pure joy this boy, this very young man.

Perhaps he is with his dad, you say to your friend. But it is ten o'clock on Thursday in London Town and he is the brightest of them all. And when the spirits come again, he is plucking the sparkler from the tray and he is holding it in his teeth and sparks are flying from his mouth as he sweeps his head and they are cheering and laughing, they are ruffling his hair.

And he must have had a few sneaky ones, you say, but the young can get drunk, so drunk, on pure joy, you think, and you remember how your cheeks shone without the help of anything when you too were young.

And the band is beaming, they are all young too, but not as young as the confident boy. And he is pushing the spirits along the table, he is leaping up and changing places and steadying a big man in his seat as he lunges forward and crashes into the table and the spirits jolt and then are still.

And the group stand to dance, swinging their arms to the music. And tonight it is Thursday, tonight they are men and the day is gone and they are held out of time in this place below the street level, held in its swaying lights and merry shouting.

And you cannot keep your eyes off this boy-man, you cannot believe that he can be so bold. You imagine him begging his dad to let him come. And his mother, you think, does she approve? You imagine him remembering this night forever in the future, the night he was one of the boys, the night the world first blazed with glory for him, the night he was a true man.

But he plays his part so flawlessly, you cannot imagine a young boy like this, unless he is very drunk. And you look closer and you see in front of him, in front of the spirits lined up, in front of the biggest glass of beer that you have ever seen, you see a glass of water.

And you long to ask someone how old he is, but you hesitate to break the spell, you hesitate because Christmas has come early, you are in a magic place, you are remembering dancing all night before you ever drank a drop, you are remembering how pure the world is, you are remembering beauty and truth and how it was before you came to this place, to this theme bar for pleasure.

And you are nearly done with your first pint and you find that you are tapping your foot to the oompah music, the corners of your mouth pulling up, and your friend is smiling as you both stare at the boy and it is too loud to speak, and you see the imp gesturing to the bar again, another tray arriving, another sparkler showering sparks from his mouth and you think he looks like an arrogant son of kings. He cannot possibly be a boy.

And you nod at your friend and you point to a two-pint beer stein on the next table and he signals the waiter – whose accent is in fact German – and you order two of the big glasses and you sit and watch the boy-child as they ruffle his hair, as one of them puts his arms around him, another slides him along the bench, for he is small and slender and light as a feather.

And you long for a tray with a sparkler, but there are only two of you.

And one of the men stands and "Are you going, are you going?" the elf shouts and you both hear his voice and it is a man's voice and you think, finally, that he must be a man.

And then his eyes catch yours and he is pointing at you and your friend and he comes round the table and he is laughing and he is slamming down two shots and his thumbs are pointing at the band and they strike up a song and you are both laughing, throwing back the red spirits, and when you look up the sparkler is in his mouth again and you feel as if your head is flying along with the sparks and you are standing and dancing, you are standing with the young imp and he is shouting, play a song, play a song, and the music is inside your head and you are young again, you are at your first wedding, you are drunk, and you cannot believe that it has arrived, this life, the life you have waited for all those years while you were growing up.

And the bell rings and the boy takes a sparkler. The men at the table are standing up and he is leading them out the door, shaking hands with the bouncers, and he is beckoning to you and your friend and you get up and follow, laughing and cheering as you stumble across the cobblestones, past Smithfield Market, all shuttered up, past Bart's, gates locked, past the silent dome of St Paul's, down to the river, to the mighty Thames.

It is mild for the last day of October and the moon is bright and the tide is high, the waves swelling and full. And beside the river wall, the men light fags and you do too and you feel like you are in your past and you draw deep and the sparks are replaced by the moon flitting off the crests of the waves and you stare out at the stumps of the old bridge, the waves touching it with a kiss before they move under the new bridge next to it, and then on.

And the lamps on the River Thames are burnishing your eyes, burning and burning your spirit-filled eyes. And you have tears in them now as you look at the young elf, laughing, laughing like quicksilver, and you watch him darting through the chattering men as they smoke fags and throw them into the dirty water. And he leaps onto the wall, laughing, bending over the waves, and they do not see him, they do not see him as they light their cigarettes and the moon swims in their eyes.

And you look at the men and back at the wall and there is only a stone cherub sitting well above the tideline, its expression hidden from you, its chubby arm pointing towards the dark river behind it. And you go closer, you hesitate, but you haul yourself up and you lean on the stone shoulder, catching your breath, lighting another fag.

And you look into the water and you cannot take your eyes off your reflection, a boy in shirtsleeves, young and slender, bursting with pride and with joy, the sparkler in his mouth arching bright flashes over the swelling river.

And you hesitate, you hesitate, but you follow him in, gasping with life at the freezing water, laughing as the bright light stretches, then folds itself below the spirited waves, laughing as you follow him down.

Laughing, until you look up and now the light is dancing far above your head. And you reach for it, desperate, you kick up, but a small hand is dragging you into the dark and as you are pulled down, the waves whispering, the waves whispering and moving on.

Drowning

H E STANDS AT the corner of the sheep pasture at dusk, the same time of day he has always stood there, watching the sun slither away from him over the hardy desert shrubs, lighting them pink, votive candles to an old way of life.

If there had been less loss, he thinks, he may have noticed the changes more, but, as it is, it has all flowed over his head and he stands as before, much the same, except for being drowned. He snorts, thinking of himself in this semi-desert, but somehow also at the bottom of the inland sea it used to be a long time ago, like the fossil of the sea scorpion stuck in hard dolomite in the *koppie* that overlooks the back yard.

He does not discount the idea altogether, although his family has only been here for two hundred years.

He imagines he can hear glacial meltwater rushing through the mountain gullies in the distance, drowning the prehistoric animals in mud. But the mountains came after the water. She had told him that. She had told him lots of things.

He goes inside and sits at the table, head in his hands,

trying not to remember her. He hears the wind sighing in the trees, like a hard broom sweeping the floor, but there are no trees here.

The trees are from that time, an age ago it feels like now, when he visited her in Durban.

The dry swishing of the broom wakes him up later that night. She is sweeping the floor again. For a moment, he can't remember whether she is dead or not.

"Why do you keep sweeping the bloody floor?" he grumbles at her, half-asleep. "I tell you, it is clean. *Skoon*."

The broom sliding over wooden planks, repeating, sliding.

He wakes at 5 a.m., tired, but he tends to the sheep, as he always has, pumping water up from the borehole into the pipe that leads to the rusty trough, scarcely acknowledging them. Their relentless need to graze makes him almost blame them for him being trapped here among the succulents that hoard their water against the harsh sun.

But he can't help feeling touched by the sight of the first rays lighting up the huge sky behind the *koppie*. Yes, it is beautiful.

He sighs. It won't last beyond six o'clock.

The borehole is not pumping as vigorously as it should. He goes to check the pipe and has to pass the small plot, marked out by crumbling posts. He wishes that he had not buried her in the graveyard at the bottom of the long pasture. And yet this had never bothered him before, all those bodies slumbering in the warm dirt, their lucky souls escaped to heaven, it had not bothered him in the least. After all, it had been the custom on his family's farm for centuries, one iron cross watching over them, that, like so many things, they had to share.

And he feels the same ill will towards the borehole as he felt towards the sheep. It is the only reason his family could settle here: there is always plenty of water deep under the ground.

In Durban, he had seen an abundance of rich life above the ground, like a vision of paradise. He felt as if she should have warned him somehow, prepared him for the flourishing greens, the sun winking through purple jacaranda flowers, and the tall palm trees. They had sat on the low branch of an enormous mahogany in her parents' back garden, the strong scent of pollinating flowers stunning him.

And she, before that, had been so excited to see the Karoo for the first time. Her family were passing through on the drive back from a holiday in Cape Town. She was the only one of them who had expressed enthusiasm for the landscape that looked uniform, but close up, he knew, had a variety of plants and animals that thrived.

"How often does it rain here?" she had asked him politely in the bar of the hotel where her family were staying overnight.

And that had been the chance he needed to explain about the low rainfall and the harsh cold of the nights in winter and the tough *witbas* bushes with their small yellow flowers, whose woody stems looked like driftwood and, although only about one metre tall, were hundreds of years old. They grew in circles around the *heuweltjies*, mounds of soft sand roughly ten metres across.

"Fairy rings," she laughed, under the watchful eye of her father, and he fell in love.

He didn't tell her that the *heuweltjies* attract deadly black mambas searching for the rodents who have a preference for the looser soil.

What he remembers most from that time in Durban is being with her in the sea – the first sea he had ever seen – salt water swelling and receding under his head, the waves shining gold as they caught the sun gliding forwards, while she stayed at his side and taught him how to float.

The thing that surprised him was that he wasn't at all scared of drowning – he felt like he could just let go, like he belonged – even though he couldn't swim.

But when he mentioned this to her, she joked that he was returning to his ancestry. She had been reading a book about the Karoo, and she explained to him that the semi-desert where he lived had once been a giant inland sea, surrounded by swampy forests and huge mammals, now extinct. His whole life, he had thought of the Karoo as something never-changing, constant, safe. Now he saw it as a speck in the flow of time.

She knew more than him about everything, chattering away in her lilting Natal English; like a pretty bird, he thought while he sat listening intently, her song washing over him, the newness of all things soaking into his skin.

In her parents' garden in Durban, creamy blossoms had showered down on their heads and they had laughed together and he had finally dared to tell her about the little birds, the Karoo chats, who mate for life.

Then she had talked about their future on his farm, all the things they would do, their life ahead. He was amazed she saw the place so differently to him, he who had known it all his life. He was amazed that she preferred it to Durban.

After the wedding, her parents posted her the book, and at night she read to him about the ancient inland sea and the strange creatures who had lived in it. Her constant chatter was like a stream of change, her white cotton dress fresh and lively as she ran up the path from the graveyard, where she liked to sit on the rocks and read, her straw hat shielding her from the sun, to kiss him when he returned home at dusk.

But something about that sea, the immense time; he started to feel so small, as if pinned down by circumstance. He couldn't quite put it into words – he longed to be on the cusp of history, to be like a body of water about to overflow into something else. His daydreams as he plodded the fields, checking fences, checking on the sheep, were all to do with water. He was trapped on solid land and when the rain came, only once or twice a year, he could not speak, although she begged him to.

And in the end, she did not share his loosening connection to the desert. The simple routines she had looked so forward to had, after all, remained simple. The problem was there was nobody, nobody at all, but her and him. She begged him to take her to town, back to the bar where they'd met, to have a child even.

He can't remember what he said, he can't remember if he said anything. And what good was any of it? It was all mere moments in time.

At last, he took her to see the rock paintings at a nearby farm. He watched as she traced her fingers reverentially in the air over the red buck and the men with bows and arrows. She seemed delighted, in love again, but she did not realise how much he had changed.

He had listened to her carefully when she explained that all people had started in Africa, that the farm workers were the same as him, that there was only one human race.

And at first, he had been surprised at how easily the hard lava of his parents' beliefs had crumbled, revealing delicate, ancient bones underneath. Later, he fretted at her lack of understanding – she did not see how much further back it all went. The Bushmen, all men, a flicker in time. She began to seem, in the unimaginably long stretch of history, insignificant. They both did.

The pipe from the borehole finally coughs out green slime in the midday heat and he goes back into the house to prepare lunch for the workers, as she used to do. But there is no bread left, only a few sacks of beans. He calls out towards the sheds, but nobody answers and he can't remember when last he saw any of them.

He sits at the table, watching the dust swirling through the open door.

He can't remember when her weeping started; it had seemed a continuation of the wind whistling across the land, something that was just there – is still there – snagging on the woody *witbas*, the wind coming inside as if to announce change, but change not coming.

He can't say when she changed from the living to the dead. Just like he can't say when his longing for her became indifference, then fear. It seemed like one long moment, the candlelight flickering over his face, caressing it, the candlelight streaming steadily over his face and a fear coming into him.

The only ghosts to fear, he thinks, are those seeking revenge. But he hadn't done anything to her. Had he?

When she died, he was already drifting. And she, like him, had wanted something.

He gets up from the table when the sun slants sideways into his eyes and goes to sit on the doorstep, looking down the path towards the graveyard. The sky is turning a dusky blue above the rapidly cooling sand, the Karoo chats singing an unintelligible yet urgent song, as if they need something, want it, demand it even.

He imagines a hand pecked through with red. 'A mean bird, a naughty bird' – that's what she would have said if she were still here, if she were . . .

"I will fly off," she'd shout. As if she had been a bird, as if she had wings.

Yes, he'd thought, one day, but it will take much longer than you think. He said nothing aloud. He did not want to talk at all by then.

On days like those, she did not look at him, or sing, or say anything. She looked down or straight ahead, anywhere so long as it was away from him.

But you have got exactly what you wanted, he'd thought.

And she had cried and swept.

When she first arrived, they had gone for walks. She pretended to be captured inside the fairy rings made by the yellow *witbas*.

"Mind the snakes, mind the snakes!" he used to say, and rush in to rescue her. But he had gradually become more concerned about possible damage to the *witbas* than to her. After all, the hardy shrubs were much older than both of them.

He goes back inside and sits down again. Her abandoned book lies on the table, dusty and dirty. He flicks through its pages. She does not need it anymore.

He can't remember what happened to her; it was a string of small changes over time, eroding . . .

She would walk out of the house, past the stunted elephant bush he had jokingly called a pretend tree, the same bush that had stood next to the path for—

She would stop near the graveyard and stare into the distance as if something might appear, something, anything.

He didn't understand what she was waiting for.

After some time – an hour, two? – she would walk back up the path.

There was nothing he could do when their love began to trickle away. And by then, he was thinking of other things. He tried to care for her, but it was like trying to hold onto the water gushing into, or draining out of, a vast inland sea.

"Rest," they'd said to her at the doctor's.

She had laughed. And he saw, for a moment, the sickness in her.

At dusk, he stands in his usual corner of the sheep pasture. How many times has he stood here? The pink is seeping into the bushes, but there is not a breath of wind and they are very still, as if waiting. It seems to him as if the desert is a vast stricken beach and the light is the sea, running away from him towards something else.

The evening grows cold. He can't hear the sheep and he realises that he has not checked on them for a while. The stars pricking the sky feel like a rebuke, something undone, unsaid; but he has never been a man of words. And yet, at the beginning . . .

A thin sliver of moon appears. How long has the moon existed in the sky, he wonders.

His memories of her sweep in, recede before they reach the shore. He wishes she could have seen things the way he does. He's glad she hadn't.

But there was something, is something, about her that he fears. What is it?

He returns to the step. It is almost dark, but he can't help looking down the path, annoyed at himself for doing so.

There was a time he had laughed happily as she danced up the stone-covered track. Now he is angry for thinking about her. She was carried away from him in time. All things must change, always.

Nonetheless, he gazes into the dark, but there is only a breeze stirring and the sound of sweeping.

She is gone and buried. And near her end she said . . . ? She said . . . ? Nothing.

He hears the rain with a dreadful clarity, hammering down from nowhere onto the tin roof of the house, the powerful scent of Durban blossoms wafting up the path.

And staring into the pitch-black, he sees, coming towards him from the graves, a white shape. A sheep? But it is too tall for a sheep.

He recognises her girlish, white dress. When last did he see her in that?

When she was young and – living.

She seems to infect the *witbas*; their slender, conserving leaves shrivel, as if they can hardly bear to absorb the rain.

"I can see the trees!" he shouts – to her?

Yes, it is definitely her, in her white dress, walking towards him up the path, tall swamp trees on either side, taller than he could ever have imagined. Better than the trees in Durban. Freakish birds sing full throttle in the dripping branches, and for a moment she is all those people, all those animals, who have ever lived – a woman in a white dress, a hunter, a sea scorpion, stone, dust – and he feels as if he is drowning.

Their song changes to the *chak-chak* of the Karoo chat. He can feel her in the rain and in the wind. And it comes suddenly like a last chance: He does not want to be drowned. He does not want the ancient inland sea. Or even Durban. He wants to live here. With her.

"We belong," he cries, "together."

The rain is deafening. He should feel joy, he should feel—

But he sees that she is part of it, of the endless slow change. In death, she is finally here, in everything.

The loneliness, unbearable, crashes in on him.

He longs for her warm skin, her special laugh, for the way she smiled at him the first time she had taken his hand. He listens for her chatter, which had somehow turned, a long time ago, into the sound of waves on a beach. But all he can hear is the rain and the harsh singing of the wind as she glides up the stony track.

At first, he can't make out her face. But as she nears, he sees that she has only dark sockets, and he remembers the human eye, how it catches a spark, how the bright white sets the centre glowing.

He longs for her to speak, to tell him what she thinks, about him, about this place. He longs for forgiveness. Or even anger.

But she does not reproach him, she does not say a word.

She glides past him into the house, as if he doesn't exist.

He stands outside in the dark and the vastness is terrifying.

She closes the door. She remains a secret, like the great cycles of life. And this is the worst thing of all.

Thin

Genesis 41:1–3 *And, behold, there came up out of the river seven well favoured kine and fatfleshed; and they fed in a meadow.*

And, behold, seven other kine came up after them out of the river, ill favoured and leanfleshed; and stood by the other kine upon the brink of the river.

And the ill favoured and leanfleshed kine did eat up the seven well favoured and fat kine.

AFTER I UNFROZE, I opened my eyes and saw five gaunt faces leaning over me and thought that everyone in this new world was starving; it turned out I was just too fat for it.

"Not thin," they said, staring down at me with disgust.

I glanced at my young slender body, then up at them: thin.

This was nothing like what we'd been prepared for. They looked like famine victims, but somehow healthy, with glowing cheeks and shiny hair. We couldn't bear to look at them.

I don't know who I'm writing this for, really; the wafers

hardly speak to us, let alone read. We're down from our original ten to five fat cryogenic freaks; as far as we know, we're all that's left of our old world. But the number five gives us a strange hope.

At first we kept asking, but they refused to explain why they thawed us; they just shook their heads at our mountains of words. We would have to speak less, they said, to practice, to get the hang of it. Of course they didn't say 'the hang'. "The thin," they said.

They put us in a white room, divided into ten sections by brightly coloured, low partitions, a futon in a matching colour for each of us.

"Go out," we said, pointing to the door.

"No space," said the guard.

He was so thin we could've pushed him out the way, but Ade said they must have some sort of hidden tech to keep us in. Besides, we all agreed it would be crowded with emaciated wafers. They wore flimsy white gowns, but ours were in lurid colours that matched our futons and they'd see us a mile off.

We never saw the guard eat or drink. Twice daily, he handed out five small squares of odourless white stuff – like manna – to each of us, then shuffled out. We sat on our futons and nibbled the squares slowly to make them last.

He updated our charts every morning, after we'd been weighed.

"Not thin," he said, shaking his head as he entered our reduced rations into the graphs above our futons. Ever so slowly, the squares got smaller as the lines on our graphs dipped downwards. It didn't seem to make him any happier.

He showed us his chart. "My original weight, ninety kg. Divide by five, my final weight, eighteen kg," he said. He pointed from his chart to ours. "Goal: weight, one-fifth."

Every ten days, a group of five wafers came to examine us.

"Strip!" they said.

We averted our faces from their grotesque bodies as they walked slowly around us, peering at our diminishing curves.

"Need more space. Special," they said.

But somehow we did not feel special. We knew they thought we were monstrous. It was the way they looked at us, bright eyes staring out from hollow sockets, like ghosts who wanted to extract the dirty secrets of our past. I'd have preferred it if they'd screamed at us, or even hit us, but all they said was "Not thin."

"Fat fucks," joked Ade after they left, the only one who seemed to find it funny.

It would've helped if they'd smiled, but by then we knew it wastes energy to smile.

They gave us crayons, ten each, in colours that matched our gowns. We sat in our white room all day and drew pictures of cupcakes and green beans and oranges. Otherwise, we compared our charts to see who was the thinnest and played Fat-Thin, a game where we listed fat things and thin things.

Ade was the first to mention it, and we all admitted it. We'd been dreaming about those children with swollen bellies, their ribs sticking out. But through their bones and stretched skin shone health. We dreamt of the wafers' gleaming, ruddy cheeks superimposed on starving African children stirring the dust in the desert.

"A moment on the lips, a lifetime on the hips," said Ade.

And I laughed in my head, but what I said was "Shut the fuck up!"

I don't know why. Maybe because he was the only one who kept talking about his children, his wife. We didn't need reminding. After all, we couldn't just hop on a plane and fly home.

We debated endlessly about what the new world looked like. Somehow, we didn't feel very excited about seeing it. We all remembered the grey ash spluttering into the sky. Anyhow, all those wafers out there would stare at us, their fat ancestors from the past, the ones they'd most probably like to forget about.

We watched each other's stomachs sink in and ribs stick out, always hungry. We lay on our futons, the bright lines on our graphs moving downwards, and wondered if the guard enjoyed seeing us disintegrate, punishing us, the not thin.

"No space," he repeated every time we brought up the door.

By the time Ade told us his escape plan, we weren't really bothered. Even if we could find food, we'd have to eat five times as much as them, like grazing cows. I lay on my futon and studied him. He was by far the fattest.

Six months after our unthawing, Ade finally decided to do it. "Before I'm too weak," he said. "I'm sure the guard doesn't have a weapon."

He saved a square a day for five days.

"Who gives a fuck?" I commented, as he grabbed his squares and pushed the guard out of the way.

We watched as he slipped sideways out the narrow door, amazed he had the energy. We saw a flash of green before the guard pushed the door closed behind him.

"Probably city lights," someone said.

They brought him back – five of them – on a stretcher.

"No corn, no wheat, no berries, no apples," he panted, his face white and gaunt against his bright purple shirt.

"Thin! Thin!" they exclaimed, loudly for them, pointing at his emaciated body. "Weight now three-fifths," they said, in what may have been excitement.

I looked at him and realised I was still so fat.

"It's pointless. They don't need us to be thin," he whispered, then fainted.

Those were his last words. We lay and watched the guard top up his drip with tiny amounts of white liquid and wondered if it was revenge.

But when he died a few weeks later, they looked puzzled.

"Not thin," said the guard, measuring our calories.

Surely we're not depriving anyone, we argued. Still, we were taking up five times as much space as anybody else.

"Four times," someone said, because we were not quite so fat anymore.

After Ade died, our dreams changed. We dreamt of ripping off our diaphanous wafer clothes and becoming fat, thick tweed and wool caressing our plump skins as we ate and drank without end. We shared them with delighted distaste.

The guard took to sitting nearby, listless, staring at the door.

One day he said, "Talk!"

It was a shock to be wanted.

We told him about our food, about cake and sausages and mashed potato, recipes and cocktails, Sunday lunch and Christmas dinner.

"Cake," the guard said. It was hard to tell, but his eyes looked brighter.

The day we stepped out . . . We woke up and the guard was sitting with his chair facing the door, and the door was open . . . In the end we just walked past him . . .

We'd imagined Tokyo or Rio.

The guard was a liar.

This is what we saw: a country field lined with oak trees, mist gently rising around their trunks, hills in the distance, and sheep, thin sheep coated in heavy wool, dragging themselves around like animated sheepskins.

"Grass, low calorie," explained the guard, before we even asked. I wanted to cry, but something stopped me: I'd never seen any of the wafers cry and it felt, wasteful.

I stroked the rough bark of an ancient oak. That tree was here when I was born, I thought. I was overcome with isolation and loneliness, and a sudden urge to kill all those unnatural sheep.

"Population, now three billion," said the guard. "No space."

I thought of the Japanese chef in the last sushi bar I'll probably ever see, his arm around my shoulder as grey ash plundered the air. We stood together and looked up at the smoke-darkened sky, the nightmare that had actually happened.

"Run!" he said.

It was only when I was halfway down the street that I realised he'd sat down.

The wafers just sort of faded away and left us to it. We were still too fat, I suppose. The guard sat in his chair all day long, only getting up to feed us. Wasted effort, really, because we hardly thought about food anymore. The next four who died just stopped eating altogether . . .

Most of the day, we lay outside under the trees, staring up into their fat branches. We noticed they had no acorns. We still had no idea why they unfroze us. After all, we were still way too fat for them.

We would never have found out if I hadn't woken early one morning, my adopted family muttering dreams in the white hush. The guard sat slumped against a wall, the light from the open door glancing off his razor-sharp cheek-bones, the wind rustling a piece of paper in his hand. I looked hard at him, absorbing the beautiful angles of his bones, like sharp points to hang the past on, something definite to aim for.

I'm almost down to weight three-and-a-half-fifths, I thought. Like Ade.

I tiptoed up behind the guard. He sat hunched over, staring at the paper, whispering a mantra again and again: "Population, one fifth of fifteen billion, now three billion. Lot space. Lot space."

There was plenty of space. But Ade was wrong. It wasn't pointless. They were helping us to get thin so we could be like them.

I looked over the guard's shoulder at Ade's last drawing: a fat man sitting at a table, butter dripping down the corner of his mouth, a scone with scarlet blobs of jam on a plate in front of him.

"Fat!" said the guard, with unmistakable admiration.

Disgusted, I watched the first tear of my new world running down his ruddy, thin cheek.

Scaffolding

These are the bones that Jack built.

I IMAGINE THE doctor works late into the night to solve my wounds. I can see he would like to crack me. I know, as in a nightmare, that he is solving not me, but an abstract problem. And when he's finished, I'll disappear again – all he can see are the wounds on the surface of my skin.

He has persistence. He would like to drill down to my bones. And when he has done it – which I have every faith he will – he'll forget about me. I'll be gone, except as a case study in the journal article that will finally make him famous. My name will be a footnote in history and no one will bother to read it.

This is the skin that lay on the bones that Jack built.
The doctor is droning on.

"Vitamin C deficiency causes open sores," he'd told me on my first visit. "Untreated, it can lead to skeletal abnormalities."

When he thought my case was simple, he couldn't wait to get rid of me. He chided me on my diet and advised me on which supplements to buy. He didn't even write a prescription.

He probably didn't expect to see me again, but I kept coming back. I had to. The doctor's lectures grew longer as the wounds on my skin and the frequency of my visits increased. I knew he thought I was wasting his time and the NHS's money, that I wasn't bothering to take the vitamins.

It was a special day for the doctor when I reported pain and swelling in my joints to accompany the deepening wounds. He took a sudden and unexpected interest in me. Well, in my body. Scurvy is virtually unknown these days, at least in Europe.

"What is happening?" I asked him, practically in tears.

He carefully explained: in cases of scurvy, the collagen maintaining scars over old wounds degenerates faster than normal skin collagen . . . or something. The scars break open. The wounds come back.

"Nothing to worry about, the vitamin C will kick in soon," he said.

"I've been taking the pills. I haven't missed one," I said.

But he still didn't believe me and arranged for me to take the vitamin C under supervision.

I do remember a moment, after he'd verified I'd swallowed the pills for several weeks, when he turned from the evidence on his computer screen and actually looked at me, properly looked.

But he ignored my tears. Or perhaps he just didn't notice them. Tears, I imagine, are not on his professional – or personal – radar. I could see the greed for knowledge shining out of him, and I knew then it was bad.

Now the way he looks at me sometimes, I feel like he is asking me something, and he doesn't know what he is asking.

This is the wound that broke the skin
That lay on the bones that Jack built.
I also don't know what the doctor is asking, but he is wearing down my patience.

The wounds kept reappearing, as if they'd never healed, as if my life was going backwards.

The doctor's real interest began when I correlated a specific wound with a childhood incident. It was a simple explanation of how the wound had occurred:

I slipped on a patch of ice and cut my hand on a jagged rock buried in the snow; it was a freezing day and nobody came – and did this make the pain a little worse?

Of course, the doctor didn't comment on my associative ramblings. His interest was not piqued by the emotions attached to the event; his initial aim was simply to find similar correlations and record them.

But the duration of my appointments increased from ten to fifteen minutes after that, then to twenty, and eventually to what felt like an eternity. I only found out much later that the doctor was neglecting his other patients and risking his job.

It was round about then that he brought up the journal paper. It was in the ideas stage, he said – in a very kind voice; of course, he needed my permission.

This is the scar
That sealed the wound that broke the skin

That lay on the bones that Jack built.

The doctor and I didn't talk about personal things at first, as is only natural in a doctor-patient relationship. Probably best, too, to avoid ripping off old scabs.

He asked me to expand on the circumstances of the incident; he needed a little more for his paper.

But "Psychologists are not doctors," he said, when I added to my original account and mentioned – impassively and factually, I thought – that I'd sustained the wound on the way home from my first, enforced visit to a psychologist. There was something wrong with me and my parents wanted it fixed.

"It's not personal," I replied, but he had turned back to his screen.

Meanwhile, my remaining scars turned red, ready to break their seals and burst open at the right moment. It's astonishing just how many scars – those unreliable wound-covers – there were on my body once I started counting.

I felt desperate. The doctor was no help. I began to match each of my wounds to its corresponding memory on my own. I needed to know the full extent of my previous injuries – that is, what the endpoint would be and how bad the pain would get before I reached it. In doing so, I became convinced the scars attached to traumatic memories were breaking open first.

Of course, I didn't tell the doctor. Given his disdain for psychology, he wouldn't have believed me.

This is the boy that made the scar
That sealed the wound that broke the skin

That lay on the bones that Jack built.
I felt like the scars were letting me down. I – my body –
had made them, but now they were failing; just another
thing I had somehow got wrong.

The doctor's interest in me intensified as even more of
my scars sprang open. I could sense his eagerness by the
way he started doing things by the book all of a sudden. I
imagined him reading an old, forgotten doctor's manual
with instructions to lean back in your chair – not too far
back – and observe the patient surreptitiously, perhaps ask
a few questions, while secretly looking for signs of mental
disturbance.

Nonetheless, the doctor remained resistant to
psychology.

I admit it was hard to get the facts straight; my memories were hazy at times. I understood how the doctor must
be feeling.

The doctor had a lot to think about as my case, and his
paper, progressed. I imagined him at home, shutting the
study door on his nuclear family to work on the article,
alone and happy in his wingback chair, his one little treat.

This is the dad with the crumpled scorn
That thrashed the boy that made the scar
That sealed the wound that broke the skin
That lay on the bones that Jack built.
It was inevitable – I realised much later – that the doctor
would ask me a personal question.

The physical evidence was overwhelming: my skin
prickled, scars blooming into wounds one after the other
like sick flowers, every single wound I'd sustained intent

on reappearing. But something was missing: the doctor needed a theory to complete his paper. And when he asked me again about the incident on the ice, I could see him turning over an idea in his mind.

Some of the wounds had, as he put it – delicately he thought – a human origin, as opposed to just tripping and falling, banging your head mistakenly on walls, doors . . . ice . . . That sort of thing. A direct human cause. Or, it might be more accurate to say, the wounds had been made by someone else, on my skin, on me. "Was there," he ventured, "somebody with you on the ice that day?"

The doctor had finally, reluctantly, entered the realm of psychology.

I rubbed my finger back and forth over one of the few unbroken scars left on my arm. There was no point in answering his question; a successful man like him wouldn't understand about my father. It would just make it harder for him to finish the article that will make him famous so that he can buy lots of wingback chairs and spend more time on his own, or with the lovely family I'm sure he has, if that is what he wants to do.

This is the mother all forlorn
That kissed the dad with the crumpled scorn
That thrashed the boy that made the scar
That sealed the wound that broke the skin
That lay on the bones that Jack built.

I was right not to answer. In our next consultation, the doctor's face fell when I inadvertently mentioned my mother. I felt such guilt for complicating things for him.

My case is something like a dead elephant I happened to see on the telly the other day: four months after the animal had been shot by a poacher, there was just a swathe of dried-out skin collapsed over her bones. There was nothing in between.

In other words, wasn't the doctor – wasn't I – leaving out something important?

The doctor was obsessed with bones. He forgot about the flesh, and all the stuff that goes with it, the feeling stuff. I can understand that better than most, although I'd rather not dwell on it.

"Any previous broken bones, or fractures?" he started asking as my wounds deepened. It wasn't just old wounds that reappeared, he explained, but also breaks in bones. "Even the bones are held together by collagen," he told me. "The bones are the scaffold of the body."

The doctor was fully committed by then, even more eager for a cure than I was. When my symptoms worsened, he admitted me to his private clinic, his sideline to the NHS. Here, people paid handsomely and the doctor always smiled.

I couldn't afford it, but he didn't charge. After all, the article was far more important than a month's worth of public school fees or extra tennis lessons. The doctor needed it to become famous and make more money.

I was starting to feel . . . dehydrated . . . dried out. I didn't want to get closer to my bones; they are, the doctor fails to understand, something best left unacknowledged. They alone, of all my tissues, escaped the early beatings and have not had to deal with any breaks. And they make things, vital things of which I have only the dimmest comprehension. Red blood cells? Corpuscles? Something, in any case, that keeps my body going.

Too distressed to read, and bored, I lay on my bed, my wounds suppurating while an IV dripped vitamin C into my arm, and made up the rhyme to pass the hours. Actually, I started it after my first visit to the doctor, but I didn't understand it and put it away for a while.

I didn't make it up, I modified it. It's one you most likely know. In my family, such as it was, it was passed from my grandfather to my father, and then to me. Maybe it started with my great-grandfather. I'm not sure how far back it goes.

I almost hoped writing it would change something. I don't know why I thought that.

I leave it next to my bed, perhaps hoping the doctor will read it. My only chance of that is if he sees it as a symptom of some kind; he wouldn't be interested otherwise. So far, nothing. I've started to use bigger, clearer handwriting.

This is the doc all tattered and torn
That noted the mother all forlorn
That kissed the dad with the crumpled scorn
That thrashed the boy that made the scar
That sealed the wound that broke the skin
That lay on the bones that Jack built.
I've realised that none of this is at all scientific and have given up hope of a cure.

The doc finally noticed my rhyme. All of a sudden, he was very interested and now he refuses to stop talking, mostly about himself. It's like he's borrowing my thoughts, telling me about how his father hit his mother, who never stopped trying to help his old dad be a better person or something. About how his mother kept telling him it wasn't his dad's fault that he hit the doc too, he couldn't help it, it was just that he'd been beaten by his father, the doc's grandfather, who had, in his turn, been beaten by his father, and so on . . . And how he finally understands that his fascination with the healing power of bones led to his medical career.

"So, perhaps worth it, in a strange way. If I could go back and choose, would I prefer to have been adopted? Would I be a doctor if I had been?" the doc asked.

I wish I could feel more compassionate, but it's my rhyme after all.

The doc stole it. There, I've said it.

The doc is still trying to finish his paper. I don't think he's in a fit enough state for it though. He seems perpetually tired.

I fed him a few facts about my early life, some true, to speed him along.

This is the patient all shaven and shorn
That treated the doc all tattered and torn
That noted the mother all forlorn
That kissed the dad with the crumpled scorn
That thrashed the boy that made the scar
That sealed the wound that broke the skin
That lay on the bones that Jack built.

After the doc finished his paper and I'd read it, I felt that he finally believed me. Once I had something definite to hold onto, I could let go, and immediately started to get better. Like anyone in recovery, I prefer not to think of the darkest days.

I'm not completely out of the woods. The paper wasn't enough for the doc. Whenever we're alone, he lies on the empty bed next to mine and asks me questions.

I wish his interrogations would stop. He can't really expect me to feel things all the time. Let go, like I did, I want to tell him.

Regardless, it's time for me to put my life back on a solid footing. My skin is healing up nicely, while the doc's has begun to show open wounds.

The doc comes into my room. He hangs his white coat on the back of a chair and lies down on the spare bed. I watch him lying there, bathed in the sterile stripes of sunlight coming through the window. I imagine his skin peeling back, splitting him open. I can feel the strands of collagen loosening, like relaxing in a bath of warm tears.

He looks into my eyes and it would almost be true, if unscientific, to say that we experience for a moment the wounds, the life, of the other, our scars small islands in oceans of pain.

But the doc is crying. He looks helpless.

I stare at the red, raw patches on his arms. And I feel that I've suffered enough. The past is the past and I want to blot it out.

The doc leaves the room to wash his face and I try on his coat. It's a good fit and I feel so secure. But when he returns and sees me, his eyes hold an incoherent question that I somehow can't bear.

I judge it best to ignore it. I need to get away. "I'm due to check out in ten minutes," I tell him.

He starts crying again.

I do have a heart. I usher him quickly into his office and seat him in the patient's chair. I whip through the filing cabinet and find a depression questionnaire, the PHQ-9 or something.

The doc bats away the form with his feeble, wound-encrusted arms. The wounds are showing down to the bones, I note.

But I know how to cheer him up. I switch on his computer. "Hang on," I say, and I google. "There are 206 bones in the human body," I tell him. "It all starts with the bones."

I Probably Am a Lonely One
(inspired by Nighthawks by Edward Hopper)

The man in the green jacket

Only the hum of electric lights as they reach across the counter for a hand, but end up with the sugar bowl or the milk. It's late and everyone is gone, except for those two, sitting together at the counter, plus the waiter and me. I push away my cold coffee and spin round on my stool to face the window, then dangle my arms, the backs of my hands brushing the cool leather, watching the people outside looking up at the sky and then disappearing round corners and into buildings. I imagine they have been beamed up to another planet and are never coming back as the light outside turns green, the inside holding its pressure, holding me in suspension, and I watch the distant lightning from my yellow bowl, my body practically hovering above the seat, electrically relaxed.

The man in the black jacket

I don't know if this woman sitting so close to me is a devil or a saint. You never know. I can only see her from the outside. She's pretty. I have the urge to take her hand.

I probably am a lonely one. I hadn't thought about it much, really. I used to hold hands and that sort of thing and then one day I thought, why? and I just let go. I hadn't felt anything much before, and I felt better right away. Although a few days later I started to wonder if there was something wrong with me and after that the loneliness came back and then I wanted to hold hands again.

It's like a mania, just something that comes over me, and I can't go in either direction. It's like, I don't know, real, a place, and all I have to do to get out is make a decision, say or do something, but I can't decide.

The woman in the red dress

In this pale yellow, the smiles of the man sitting next to me are pale too – not quite directed at me, but past me, and past the whirling dervish inside me that he can't see. I feel as if I need to be plugged in, as if I'm missing a socket. I need something – someone – to make my hair stand on end.

I feel like weeping. I feel a lot of things. They're all in here. What good would it do to tell him? Or anyone?

I tell myself it will all be better tomorrow.

The man in the green jacket

The people outside have all disappeared, before the rain comes down, as if obeying some hidden electric signal.

Do those two over there even know each other?

I glance at them from my stool as I hover, suspended, and I feel . . . I feel . . . not happy, not that. Safe. Much better. I am held by soft light, and because I am held, I can watch the lightning splitting the distant horizon and I can veer off into eternity.

The man in the black jacket
I wish that I could speak to her. Just one word, just one, and we could turn round and look out of the window together, or maybe get married (in time, of course), get to know each other's realities. I wish I could find the right smile, touch her hand, something to make a spark, but you need two things together, don't you?

The woman in the red dress
I look directly at him and gesture to the sugar bowl. He passes it to me and I feel myself sinking as his lips press together, then open, still no words coming out, and it is worse, far worse, than if I'd never tried at all. My hopes were so small – unrealistic in retrospect (and secretly so big).

But his hand is close to mine.

The man in the green jacket
Those two over there with their backs to the first drops of rain. I almost want to call out, I almost want to say it: Hey! Look at the sky splitting!

But they only sneak looks at each other, each time the thunderclaps sound louder.

The man in the black jacket
I imagine she is called Mary, that she has a nice place with nobody in it, except silence. I imagine her with a husband, three children. Why would she need anybody else?

My hand lies on the counter, palm on the cool surface, miles apart from hers, our fingers almost touching.

The man in the green jacket
The thunder outside is loud now, crashing against the green, and it's like each clap is expelling something into white light, slicing the sky apart.

The woman in the red dress
Let's talk about it. Let's talk! Let's listen. Let's hold hands and squeeze, even if we don't understand each other, until real fascination takes over and we forget that we are trying. Let's feel each other's feelings, be the other for a day, a moment. Let's be lonely together – and we both know what that's like. Let's be together.

The man in the green jacket
The rain is really coming down now. Look at those two over there, not even noticing the weather!

I'm not like them: I hold my secrets in my own hands. I've been in love, I just prefer to dream alone.

I look back out of the window as a huge fork of lightning strikes the ground and a ball of light springs from it and rolls across the sky towards us.

"Hey," I shout to the two of them, to the waiter, the words strange in the smooth, thick silence. "Hey!"

They turn slowly, not expecting much, and I point to the luminous white ball bouncing across the street, its edges indistinct.

The man grips the woman's hand, and they gasp and smile at each other with wide open faces.

The waiter flicks off the light. It is green and dark and eerie, and then we are anointed.

The lighting ball floats in like a dream, over the low sill, through the big window opened outwards against the rain, and weaves between us, its edges barely holding together.

The man in the black jacket
"Unbelievable!"

The woman in the red dress
"Oh!—"

The waiter
"Watch out!"

The man in the green jacket
After they leave, I'm the only one here, except for the waiter. He smiles at me and goes on drying glasses and we sink back into silence. Cool air blows the smell of rain through the big window and I can't stop thinking about the lightning ball – a single touch would have been fatal, but it was so beautiful.

It floated among us, and I wanted to hold on to it for the rest of my life . . . It had all these things in it. But how could it last? It only stayed together for a moment, and I was left with shadows of blue and green playing on my face as it bounced back into the street, the sky, and disappeared.

Wolphinia

I T USED TO be that I didn't dare stop driving around – people would notice; I'd make them feel guilty and they might attack. Now on my walks through the harbour, all I have to do is duck the cars that smash through the barrier high above my head. And flinch when they hit the heap of metal that lines the sea wall.

Ride not riot. That's the tiny government's latest slogan. Not that anyone's listening since the election turnout dropped to 2.3 percent. But the people keep queueing up for their petrol. Fucking lemmings!

I follow the harbour wall that ends at the old customs house, tucked underneath the flyover, now the seat of the tiny government. I'm wondering what they actually do, besides doling out petrol, when out of the mucky water pops this wolphin and I jump a fucking mile.

I put my hands up. Wolphins aren't stupid. It's very likely to be pissed off: every time another car 'forgets' to take the curve and flies off into the sea, a wolphin floats belly-up afterwards.

Still, what on earth do I expect it to do? Gun me down? Wolphins don't have hands.

I look closer. It's way too big to be a British wolphin. Maybe the rumours were true, maybe it's ex-Russian. Not that anybody cares. Even the Nationalists have given up – more important fish to fry and all that.

The wolphin half-rises from the waves and opens its mouth, as if it's struggling to say something. I'm interested. Conversation is pretty scarce these days. I edge closer, keeping my hands up, but the wolphin moves back. You can't blame it for being suspicious – I am a human, after all.

Though hardly anyone's fishing anymore. Even the police just drive around. To be fair, there's not a lot else left to do.

Whistle, whistle, goes the wolphin, and it flips over and wiggles its tail.

I wasn't too hot at Wolphinese when everyone was into it – before the wolph-fishing started. Anyhow, I don't even know if it speaks Wolphinese, let alone English.

I sneak a look at its undercarriage, but I can't tell if it's F or M. Oh well, nobody gives a shit since the babies stopped coming. It probably can't tell about me either: I've shaved my hair off now Mom's not around to tell me to act like a proper girl.

I'm trying to remember 'hello' when another wolphin swims up, a big grin on its face. Well, it's hard to tell, really, when a wolphin is smiling.

Maybe it's for the best I don't speak Wolphinese: the fanatically fluent were the first to start eating their new friends.

I put on a lame grin and lower my hands.

Whistle, whistle, goes the first wolphin again, and the second hesitates, then rolls over.

Fuck me! It's got little hind legs.

I'd read about this during the wolphin craze. Super-rare. And these ones look like proper legs – like they might actually be going somewhere – not like the tiny buds in the pictures.

I'm literally at a loss for words, but I want the wolphins to know that I would never eat them – unlike some, I recognise their official person status. I'm not a fucking cannibal! I look towards the concrete bunker of the tiny government and flip the finger, and I spit afterwards for good measure. The wolphins do a little jump and I know they understand. They start to swim away, but then they turn and look back at me and I wish I could go with them.

But I can't. Sure, I'm a little mercury toxic already, but it'll be swiftly over if I so much as touch that water.

I can't even say 'tomorrow' in Wolphinese, so I point to the sun, then roll my hands, and they do another jump.

I watch them swim out to the harbour mouth. I wonder if they've managed to get anywhere beyond this crappy island.

I meander in the direction of the customs house. The tiny government blew the remains of the budget on bullet-proof window glass and fenced off the last working petrol pumps – conveniently located next to the customs house. Word has it, they even recruited a few ex-Russian wolphins to protect them on the ocean approach. Hush hush, of course: the soldier wolphins were officially all home-bred British. Fucking Nationalists.

There's a ripe breeze coming from the cars that didn't make it into the water. I pull my scarf up over my mouth as I stare out to sea. It looks almost beautiful, a grey gleam catching the sunshine through a break in the clouds. But I know what's in that water.

Still, plenty of fish in the sea, if you don't mind eating just a little mercury.

The wolphins frolic in the dim sunlight, a bit creaky, but basically survivors – the new roaches of the sea, as their ex-friends, the Wolphinistas, took to calling them, just before they started eating them.

No one would dare eat them now: they are packed to the gills with mercury. But somehow thriving – like the tiny government is rumoured to be. Everybody used to want to know their secret, when they still cared about living forever.

I pull out a cigarette. Mom and Pops went on and on about it, before they started the big drive, but, really, my lungs can't tell the difference. I lift up my scarf and take a drag and pretend to blow the smoke out through the top of my head, like a wolphin.

The tiny government hasn't been sighted outside their bunker for some time, except for their petrol people doling out the rations.

I cough in surprise as a school of wolphins swims right past me – at least forty. They roll over and wiggle their legs. They all have the legs! Except for the leader, who I take to be the first wolphin I met. They clear their blowholes and swim in formation in the direction of the tiny government.

Once, I would have run to tell someone the news . . . Now I just stare. Who is there to tell?

But it's a bit like old times. I haven't seen a wolphin parade since the wolph-fishing started. As far as I was concerned, conscripting them was cruel, more soldiers for the useless cause. God knows what they were actually making them do.

The wolphins surface way past the customs house and swim back out to the harbour mouth.

I can't help wondering what they're up to. Do they have a plan? Or are they just stupid, great fake fish in the pay of the tiny government?

Still, what would they pay them with? Wolphins don't need petrol, and even if they could drive, they're already in the sea.

Whatever. I may as well try and find out. I don't exactly have anything else to do.

It'd be less suspicious to get close to the customs house in a car, and I'm sort of regretting my resolution to give up driving. But there are a few people who approach on foot if they're dumb enough to run out of petrol . . . Usually women, according to the government.

I never thought I'd count myself lucky to be a girl. How could I when the tiny government are all men? It's kind of a sicko joke now that women are crashing through the barriers into the sea in equal numbers.

But I'm not stupid enough to just walk right up to the bunker empty-handed. I'll have to go home for some props.

◊

It's been a while since I've seen the house. The dead telly reflects slices of yellow grass between the window slats. Mom and Pops used to spend a lot of time watching the news; later, they just watched the crashes.

I run upstairs to their room, grab one of Mom's wigs

and Pop's binos, and run back down to the kitchen. I'm ravenous.

I open the cupboard and stare at the tins and tins of fucking fish.

"Eat your little fish, Monkey," I hear Mom saying, and I force myself to move on to the garage.

I fling a rusty petrol can into the back seat of the saloon.

The keys are in the ignition. I haven't driven my car since Mom and Pops sailed into the harbour, in a manner of speaking. I start the engine and collapse against the wheel, laughing. When I remember that mood incongruence is one of the early mercury symptoms, I laugh even more, until I'm weeping. Eat your little fish – what's a little poison on the side? Mom and Pops couldn't help it. What else was there to feed me? Ha ha ha!

I hoot and wave at my one remaining neighbour as I cruise past. Once, she would have been so proud I'd started driving again. Now she doesn't even look up. She just carries on checking the petrol in her tank.

It's dusk by the time I get back to the harbour. I drive right past the bunker. Hopefully I'll pass as just another petrol junky, desperate for my next ration. I scan the sea as I take the entrance to the flyover.

I'm not supposed to stop up here, but it's almost dark. I pull over to the shoulder, where I can get a good view of the customs house. Just in time, it turns out. A small van accelerates through the hole in the barrier and lands way out. Talk about making a big splash!

I aim Pop's binos at the bunker to avoid looking at the red stain spreading across the water. I can tell it's blood, not petrol. The van must have hit a wolphin. And that's when I see the dinghy heading out from the customs house.

I didn't know there were any boats left. It's even got an engine. Three MPs crouch in it, holding a long pole with a hook on the end. They snag the wounded wolphin as soon as it surfaces.

What the fuck? Its best chance is to be left alone. People know about the self-healing power of wolphins – that's what got them started on eating them. And it's the tiny government that banned wolph-fishing in the first place, once they realised about the mercury. Maybe they are trying to save it?

The wolphins surround the dinghy and start jumping out of the water. They almost knock the pole off the boat, but the MPs speed back to the bunker and haul the wolphin out onto the fenced-off slipway. It makes a strange, strangled scream and tries to thrash free. They deliver a swift booting, and I know for sure that they are not going to save it. They drag it hurriedly through the big metal doors, to the answering screams of its fellow wolphins.

Fuckers.

I can't stop thinking about Mom and Pops on their final trip into the harbour. Did they even remember me before the big crash?

Whatever.

I sit until it's almost dark, watching Mom and Pop's mascot wolphin swinging from the car mirror. They used to worship the wolphins for being mercury tolerant, but in the end they were jealous.

I'm badly tempted to just keep on driving.

I roll the car forward until it blocks the gap in the

barrier, pull on Mom's wig, get out, and throw the keys over the edge.

I feel my way down the flyover, one hand on the barrier, petrol can in the other.

A weak moon lights up the dirty mist floating over the harbour. I imagine the wolphin ghosts, torn and twisted, rising healed from the water – like Jehovah's Witnesses on resurrection day – and marching back onto the land, while the humans drop into the gloom, trailing red, clutching their precious steering wheels.

I put down the petrol can, then creep towards the bunker. I make it to the wall that runs at right-angles to the sea. I inch along it, before I notice the MP sluicing wolphin blood from the dinghy tied to the inside of the fence that juts out from the wall into the water. I press myself against the wall until he goes back in.

I turn around slowly. A small circle of light is showing through a hole in the blackout cloth over the only window. I have to stand on tiptoe to peer through.

Luckily, the MPs have their backs to me. They're sitting at a long table, watching a tall man. He stands facing them, eyes closed, hands uplifted, doing some sort of prayer, it looks like. There's an enormous white plate in front of each of them. I strain closer until I see that telltale black meat with the red edges, like hot and angry coals. Wolphin meat.

I turn and shuffle away as fast as possible, my hand over my mouth.

Fucking cannibals!

I wish those wolphins would reappear. I need somebody to talk to. Nothing makes sense. Not because the MPs are eating wolphin – you never know what to expect from humans. It's because I realise that there is not one sane person left.

Why am I so surprised?

I crouch by the wall until the night smudges into another grey day, half hoping the wolphins won't come. I've never touched even a sliver of wolphin meat, but how will they know that?

The wolphin surfaces alone. I don't expect sympathy after its companion has just been offed by its supposed fellows. But I remove Mom's wig. I want it to recognise me. I want it to know that not all humans are the same.

"Sorry," I say, and it does its little jump.

And it makes everything worse. I stand looking away from it, pressing my sleeve against my stupid mouth, trying not to laugh. Fucking mercury! I'm losing it!

"Sorry, sorry," I say, and I look it straight in the eye and almost reach out to stroke its shiny, poisonous flank, the red tip of its sore fin. I almost do. But I can't. Even a few drops of water on my skin will . . . But what difference . . .

The wolphin whistles at me, then turns its nose to point at its fin, then whistles again. My eyes have gone all blurry. All I can think of is Mom and Pop's last drive, and I realise I'm crying . . . Better than laughing, I suppose.

It whistles again and I wipe my eyes. When I see what is wedged between its fin and body, I finally understand what it's trying to tell me.

I look up, trying to clear my head. The school of wolphins have gathered at the harbour mouth and are swimming patterns in the water; it feels like they are showing me the way when they roll over in unison and wave their stubby legs.

I understand what it's like to be them, I understand what it's like to be ignored. What did the tiny government ever do for us?

I take off my scarf and wrap it round my hand. I lean down and gently lift up the grenade.

Pops was ex-military, like almost everyone since we became disconnected from the continents and there was no longer any cause. He used to tell me tales about kamikaze Russian wolphins. "They couldn't get the English ones to detonate the grenades," he'd whisper.

I'm pretty sure he never dreamt I'd be dumb enough to try it one day. Even if I was a girl.

But now I'm finally a young woman. I breathe out. What next?

I know already. I point towards the bunker, towards the remains of that feeble atrocity, the tiny government. "Now?" I ask, and the wolphin jumps up high.

My fingers are so numb that I let the scarf fall and hold the grenade with my bare hands. I can't help flinching as the drops of water touch them, but I've got a feeling I won't be needing them soon.

I'm shivering as I clasp the grenade and sneak over to the bunker wall. No sign of any MPs. I unbutton my shirt and tuck the grenade inside, then clamber along the fence and swing myself round to where the dinghy is tied up.

The hardest part is getting into the boat. I can't stop trembling at the thought of all that water. Maybe Pops was right: those Russian wolphins must have been nuts to blow themselves up.

But then, they didn't have a good reason.

The dinghy rocks from side to side as I untie it, get in,

and use the pole to push it close enough to the open metal doors.

The MPs stare at me as I bob into their line of sight.

The wolphins know that I'll die in that water. And I now know for sure I will never join them when they march back out onto the land.

I may as well make myself useful.

"For Mom and Pops," I yell, as I pull the pin and lob the grenade straight through the doors.

There's a bright flash, and I feel strangely illuminated from the inside out as I'm blown through the air into the poisonous sea.

◊

The wolphins push me up to the surface to breathe, and the feeling of being carried aloft on their little hind legs almost makes up for the fact that it's nearly all over for me.

Now that the tiny government is wolphin food, my rage has gone. The grey water actually appears blue and fresh. An obvious delusion, but I have to admit, I'm enjoying it.

At least it's better than just driving around.

A, *and I*

23 September 2026, 'real' mood: I don't know.
Forced to start writing an online 'mood diary' when *A*
arrived two days ago. Psych insisted. Part of the experiment, she said. OK, I said. Easier than arguing. And three
weeks off work.

As if that wasn't enough, she told me about the latest
theory of emotions: we have twenty-seven of them.
Apparently. She showed me the emoji set and said to 'stick'
the one that best describes how I feel in the diary each day.
And add a few notes about my feelings. An old-fashioned
and horrible idea!

I told her I preferred the previous theory of just six
emotions. Hmm . . . deflection, she said.

So, I am writing this *proper* diary on the side, a full
account. On paper, where Psych and her eager research
crew can't get hold of it. I'll have to hide it from *A*. He's
supposed to be clever. So far, I can't see much evidence of
that!

Psych says my reluctance to 'journal' is down to repression. At our prep session for *A*'s arrival, she let it slip – in
a Freudian manner, ha ha – that she thinks my resulting

emotional projection is one of the most severe cases she's come across, at least in this age of open psyche. She tried to cover up her slip by saying repression was quite common in the past.

We often discuss my repression, but I had no idea she thinks I'm among the best of her worst cases – a super-projector!

She seemed proud of me. Who knows though? She's hard to read, being a psych. They are the only ones left who thankfully keep their feelings to themselves.

The main task ahead, she said, was for me to learn to identify my emotions. I could tell she was very excited.

When *A* arrived with his minder, he looked just like any other neuromorphic android. As soon as I saw him, the phrase '*A, and I*' popped into my head and I wanted to laugh.

Laughter under stress. Unconscious deflection of emotions, Psych would say. Then she'd ask, how do you feel, and I'd shrug. There'd be no point in saying, I don't know, yet again.

In any case, I couldn't laugh because the woman from PsyRo was standing right there, looking very serious. And a little anxious? Any questions? she said. I wanted to ask how intelligent *A* was. I didn't. She'd only think I was overcomplicating things.

Have fun, she said.

A hadn't said a thing, not even hello. After they left, I invited him into the kitchen. He sat himself down at the table.

I'm *I*, I said, trying not to giggle.

He didn't answer.

Can I call you *A*? I asked.

He continued with the silent treatment. Did he get the joke?

The PsyRo leaflet said his default name was Jeff, but I could change it to whatever I wanted.

Hi, Jeff, I tried, but he didn't respond to that either.

I'll just call you *A*, then, I said.

Does he mind?

Hard to tell.

Of course not! Robots can't feel.

24 September 2026, 'real' mood: I don't know. Ha ha.
Forgot to do the emoji yesterday. Unconscious resistance, Psych would say. Easy to catch up: I closed my eyes and touched the screen at random. My finger landed on 'nostalgia'. Odd, if harmless. So I said I was nostalgic for the days before I started therapy and hadn't been told anything was wrong with me yet. Can they tell I only stuck it in today? Probably. Doesn't matter – if so, it'll become part of their study.

Meanwhile, back at the ranch, *my* ranch, *A* just sits in the kitchen, looking almost real – a buff, scruffed-up Action Man type. Still find it hard to believe he's intelligent. I bet he's an old model. Psych and her mindy mates probably clubbed up to buy him at a sale. I bet their practice is dwindling as it's becoming the norm to let it all hang out. Difficult to tell though, until he talks. He may yet surprise me!

Anyway, I suppose we both know why he's here, even if, in his case, it's programmed into him.

25 September 2026, 'real' mood: Who knows? I don't. Ha ha HA!

I didn't have to agree to this. I wish I hadn't. I don't even want to mention endless yesterday, sitting through three meals opposite an elective mute. *A* is a waste of money! I'm sure a houseplant, or any other inanimate object, would be just as effective. Obviously a lot cheaper too!

I reread the PsyRo leaflet. *A* is an autonomous learner. Apparently. How is he going to learn anything if he chooses not to speak?!

Psych explained that *A* is supposed to stop me super-projecting: Projectors offload their unwanted feelings onto others. For example, you think someone is angry with you, but you are really angry with them. *A* won't react back emotionally (countertransference), like a human would, and eventually I'll have to 'own' my feelings.

I think I've got it right? A neat little theory. But really?! I'm still not convinced. If *A* wants to sit in my kitchen all day saying fuck all, silently blaming me for having to be here, then that's fine with me.

Had a thought: is *A* cross with me, perhaps for calling him *A*?

Bit later

Just went to open the back door for *A* so he could look out at the autumn leaves to calm himself down. Felt sorry for him, all cross and alone. He continued to stare at the wall.

I'm thinking of turning him off.

He's hardly likely to have a switch. Imagine if you could switch off people!

26 September 2026, 'real' mood: Tired. Is tired a mood?
Went to bed at usual time. Was almost asleep when I thought, is sleep like being switched off? Couldn't sleep after that, thinking about *A* sitting in my kitchen, probably wanting to turn me off! Is he still angry with me? And/ or dangerous?

I fell asleep in the early hours and had a weird dream. *A* was standing next to my bed, unsmiling, with a tray of tea and toast. He looked – as in life – so real. I thanked him, but he didn't reply.

Woke up feeling gritty and dirty and desperate for caffeine. Went downstairs and *A* was sitting there, brooding on how boring this all is, no doubt, staring out the back door. The back door was open! I locked it before going to bed. Mixture of relief he's actually moved and worry about the back door being open. Is he trained to repel attackers too? I'll email Psych after this and ask.

27 September 2026, 'real' mood: I don't know.
Avoid deflection, go with it, Psych replied. The only other thing she said was, don't forget the emojis. She didn't even ask how I was.

Realised I'd forgotten the emojis again. Fetched laptop and opened 'Journal'. Closed my eyes. My finger landed on 'amusement' and 'interest'.

Does Psych know what she's doing?

It's OK, trust takes time, I hear her voice. Not exactly soothing, but calming, like an enormous mother cat with its claws voluntarily sheathed. I'd run a mile if she ever got them out. Perhaps she knows that? What if she is really a bad person, hiding behind something else – knowledge?

Why doesn't she show me HER emotions? What if she is projecting her feelings onto me and I was fine all along?

27 September 2026, second entry for today, 'real' mood: ? Who gives a shit? Ha ha.

Had an idea after another lunch with the speechless man, I mean robot, ha ha. (I wish he could eat. Anything to dull the monotonous silence.) I was thinking about Psych and I remembered that framed photo of her cat. I only noticed it on my third visit. A curiously cowlike specimen – white with black spots, which it obviously didn't earn itself. It sat looking straight into the camera. Nothing remarkable about it except for the spots. I was staring at it when suddenly I found myself telling Psych about my mother's cats.

I don't think I gave too much away. Though, since *A*'s arrival, I'm starting to understand how even a sentence can reveal quite a lot. Theoretically.

So, I remembered the psych's spotted cat, and cats are the number one Internet marketing lure. Ninety-nine percent of humans can't help going gaga when they see one. (Not me. I'm in the one percent. Not allergic or phobic – just indifferent.)

I got out my phone and found the cutest, most popular cat pic I could: a tabby kitten in a Christmas hat. I walked round the table and stood between *A* and the open back door. Say what you like about him, he's a creature of habit. I dangled the phone in front of his face. Kitten, I said. Needlessly. I'm sure he 'knows' what a kitten is. But he stopped looking at my stomach – which was blocking the view – and stared at the screen. For a long time! Who knows what was going through that supposedly superior mind of his?

If you ask me, I'd say he's stupid, but the leaflet says he can outpace me effortlessly in his logical processing.

Still, robots can't feel.

I finally took my phone away. *A* went back to staring out the door, even when it started pouring down outside.

Was this mean of me?

He CAN'T feel!

28 September 2026, 'real' mood: Jury's out.

Bloody Psych! Are you happy now? I finally feel something.

When I said good morning, *A* just kept staring out the open back door. It was too much and I locked him in the downstairs bathroom. Opened it briefly to shove in my phone with the kitten picture open. Locked it again.

I just wanted him to say something. Maybe cry out to be rescued? He didn't even try the handle.

I sat at the kitchen table in his chair. Couldn't stop worrying about him.

When I unlocked the bathroom after three hours, he was still staring at the kitten pic. Sorry, I said, and he handed me the phone. He looked sad.

I feel bad (no emoji for that!). I'd never lock a person in a bathroom.

Note to self: *A* is not real, remember! He doesn't feel. He can't, despite his – almost – lifelike exterior.

29 September 2026, 'real mood': Ha, fucking ha!

Same dream last night: *A* stood next to my bed with the

tray of tea and toast. I thanked him. He smiled at me, but didn't reply.

No idea what this means.

I woke up and went downstairs. *A* was sitting on his chair in the kitchen. Not smiling.

Good morning, *A*, I said, brightly.

He didn't answer, and I didn't care at all.

Of course I didn't offer him any Fakin-Bacon. I laughed to myself – an internal state unique to humans – at how he'd smiled in the dream despite himself, as I layered the crispy strips onto my toast.

30 September 2026, 'real' mood: Thoughtful.

I thought, for the first time, what is *A* doing in the night while I sleep? Out gathering cats perhaps? Ha ha! He's still obsessed with the kitten pic.

I'm sure there's a way to power him down, a command probably. I will email Psych and ask.

1 October 2026, 'real' mood: I don't know.

Psych's reply was unhelpful: please confine your questions to urgent matters.

If she wants to act so unprofessionally, then so be it!

Is she punishing me for not saying much all these years? After all, a psych needs a patient to speak. It must be very boring otherwise!

I'm sure she's a bit angry. Perhaps she should get herself an anger-management robot. Ha ha!

Had an idea. *A* is so attached to the kitten pic, I could get him his own phone. Maybe it'll force him to say thank you. No, I've just thought of something much better! I don't know if it's allowed, but no one has explained what I can or can't do, so I'm going to do it.

2 October 2026, 'real' mood: Excited! I think?

I've broken the rules! If there are any. I took the high-speed tram and came home with a kitten. A tabby kitten.

A said nothing as I lifted the kitten out of the basket. Quelle surprise! *But* I did catch a startled look on his perfect face. A third expression to add to the two he has shown so far. I put down the kitten's basket, shook some litter into its tray, and went upstairs to find a blanket. And when I came downstairs, *A* was bent over, stroking the kitten. Kitty, kitty, he said.

I was gobsmacked. It worked! I'd made him speak!

Is this what Psych feels like when she gets me to artic-ulate an emotion?

I tiptoed out and left them to it.

Does *A* feel?

No!

3 October 2026, 'real' mood: ?

Had the dream again. *A*, next to my bed, with the tray of tea and toast (if only!). Like before, I thanked him. This time, he openly grinned at me, but still didn't reply. I felt frustration whipping through me like a hurricane (is frustration an emotion?). Speak, I whispered, but his grin just got wider. He looked like a demented clown. Speak, I shouted. But he didn't.

I jerked awake. I went downstairs. As usual, *A* was sitting in his chair, staring out the back door, with the kitten in his arms. Did he pick it up? Or did it jump there, not realising of course that *A* can't feel?

I am human and can feel, but I am also – according to the psych – too rational. After years of failed attempts at self-improvement, I finally wonder if she has a – slight – point.

We need to try something new, she told me, after a particularly gruelling session about my mother's cats. (How I wish I'd never mentioned them. I blame her cow-spotted familiar for that.)

I sat opposite her in the flowered wingback chair and imagined myself spilling over, like the cream off the top of the milk my mother used to pour for her cats at breakfast. Before we were allowed the leftovers for our tea.

If I didn't address my emotions, I would explode, Psych continued.

Personally, I saw no signs whatsoever of this impending explosion, but she looked so upset, I was worried she'd start crying and accepted her plan to try *A*.

She said he was a bit like a therapy pet, but far more sophisticated. Then she composed herself and gave me one of her raised-eyebrow, but calm, looks. Perhaps she should have been a robot, ha ha.

Not true, she is a very feeling person, I can tell, even though she obviously can't share her feelings with me in therapy. Sometimes, I wish we were friends. I have even had the occasional urge to invite her down the pub.

Not so sure now. I wouldn't be surprised if she's unconsciously cross with me for abandoning her for *A*. Perhaps she wants me to say how I feel about *her*?

Either way, I'm sure she misses me!

4 October 2026, 'real' mood: Why don't they increase the number of mood emojis then perhaps I'll be able to fucking identify one properly!

A and the cat – kitten, I should say – seem to have formed a close bond, even though *A* is *not* human and *can't* feel.

Went downstairs. *A* was in his chair. The back door was closed. I opened it. Look at the trees, I said, but *A* was looking down at his lap, and I noticed the kitten snuggled against his – very realistic – muscled, T-shirted stomach.

Cold, he said to it, stroking its fur. Beautiful, soft, he said.

I felt – ? Something complex. I don't know how to describe it. I felt something, anyway.

If this is what the psych was trying to get me to do, I don't like it!

Maybe *A* is programmed to stroke cats?

5 October 2026, 'real' mood: Glum.

Love that old word. Love a lot of old things: family, friends, stability of weather patterns on Mother Earth. Seek a mother in yourself, Psych always says, but I think she's having a laugh. She's never met my mother's cats!

Only joking.

Stuck the right sticker, 'sadness', into the mood diary today by mistake. Does that make it true? I prefer 'glum'. Glum, sad, despondent, what's the difference?

Am I 'owning' my feelings?

Yes. Yes!

One, anyway.

Should I call Psych and tell her I've matched a 'real' feeling to the emoji chart?

What's the point? She'd probably just say I haven't felt enough yet.

A talks to the kitten all the time now. His vocabulary is expanding rapidly: cutey, sweetie, beastie, cuddles, etc. And he can't stop feeding it milk.

Is *A* lonely? Is he programmed not to talk to me? I'm going to email the psych and ask.

6 October 2026, 'real' mood: Glummer, Glum-er?
Focus on your own feelings, please, Psych replied.

I feel like an utter, awful, fucking something or other. Find that on your chart, I want to email back, but won't.

Still, Psych has a point: It would be a waste of time to focus on *A*'s feelings. *A CAN'T FEEL.*

Wrote one line in the 'Journal'. Didn't add an emoji. Couldn't find one for utter, awful, etc. I'm sure Psych will reprimand me. I don't care. There should be a sliding scale of emoji stickers for glumness – ending in death. Perhaps I should email *that* to the psych. Ha ha ha!

I'm writing this on my lap in the kitchen. The back door is open and the last of the red leaves are twirling off the trees. *A* and the kitten are playing together in the living room. I'm going to try to imagine I have no feelings. I'm going to imagine I'm *A*.

Not working. All I can see is my mother pouring the rich cream into her cats' saucers, while we wait for our breakfast.

Does Psych secretly hate me? Does *A* secretly hate me? Even if he can't feel?

7 October 2026, 'real' mood: I don't know. Calm? Is calm a mood? Why can't it be, if not?

Today, I'm calm enough to know I'm not that calm.

Had the dream again. *A* with tray, toast and rogue-clown grin. Still not speaking. I refused the tray, and *A* leant down next to my bed and poured the cream from *my* milk into the saucer for *my* tea and fed it to the kitten.

Why can't dreams just tell you their message in plain English?

Went downstairs. *A* was on the kitchen floor on all fours, facing the kitten. He jumped straight up into the air (amazing, inhuman agility) and the kitten mimicked him! It wasn't a fluke. They repeated it three times. Then *A* gave the kitten some milk.

Why didn't evolution discourage feeling mammals from being unwittingly attracted to robots? *A* is one hundred percent rational. Why would a kitten be attracted to that?

8 October 2026, 'real' mood: Fuuuuck!

Decided to feed the kitten myself. Went downstairs and caught *A* in the act of separating the cream off the top of the milk and pouring it into the kitten's saucer. Maybe he rang my mother for advice, ha ha!

9 October 2026, 'real' mood: ???!!!

Was watching TV last night while *A* and the kitten played on the rug. Ignored them, like they were ignoring me. *A* said, roll. Out of the corner of my eye, saw the kitten dutifully rolling over. Perhaps *A* is projecting his alleged intelligence onto the kitten, ha ha. Carried on watching TV.

10 October 2026, 'real' mood: ? I don't know, but I can feel it.

Was watching the news and noticed *A* and the kitten at the table. *A* had my laptop open. He beckoned me over (a first). His expression was neutral.

I went over – reluctantly – and he and the kitten were watching a NewTube video. The thumbs-up icon was pinging madly. *A* pressed replay: The video started with *A* jumping into the air on all fours, copied by the kitten wearing a miniscule Christmas hat on its tiny head. Then *A* said, roll, and the kitten rolled over. It ended with *A* pouring cream into *my* saucer as the kitten lapped it up.

Is the kitten going to grow up to be like my mother's cats?

Locked *A* and the kitten into the bathroom. Sat in *A*'s chair for five minutes before kitten mewed. Immediately let both of them out. Neither of them looked at me. God knows, I deserve it. They must be furious.

Had a thought: perhaps I should email Psych and ask if the kitten is allowed to live here?

11 October 2026, 'real' mood: Glum.

Go with how you feel, Psych replied.

After yesterday, I'm even less convinced this is a good idea.

Had a thought: perhaps the kitten is too dumb to realise *A* is not real and can't feel?

Do cats project?

12 October 2026, 'real' mood: Glum.

I can't wait to return to work.

13 October 2026, 'real' mood: Glum.
I'm beginning to wonder if *A* would prefer an autonomous life in his own home. And what that might look like. Perhaps with the kitten as a companion?

14 October 2026, 'real' mood: Hate. Definitely hate!
Had the dream again last night. *A* came in with tea and toast and the kitten sitting – incongruously – on his shoulder. His smile was moderate and calm, just like Psych's. He put down the tray. Speak! I screamed. He answered straight away. I hate you, he said, in an eighties style robotic voice.

Managed to evade *A* and the kitten by busying myself upstairs all day, then creeping out the back door. Left it open. I was sure *A* would close it, or not, as he liked. Found a pub and sat in a quiet corner to avoid talking to anyone. Wanted to work out the meaning of the dream. Seemed to be saying that *A* hates me. But dreams are not straightforward. And robots can't feel.

Drunk several pints past my limit. Went home after closing. Found *A* teaching the kitten how to stand on its hind paws and extend a forepaw in a handshake. The laptop was open to their video. The two of them had millions of thumbs ups and had gone viral.

I hate you both! I screamed. I ran to the bathroom, with my diary, and locked myself in for the night.

15 October 2026, 'real' mood: Sore head. Sore, sore, sore.
Sore, sore, sore head! Woke up shivering on cold bathroom floor. 5 a.m.! Crawled upstairs to avoid *A* and kitten. Email from Psych saying they are coming to get

A at 3 p.m. Traitor! He must have sent her a message. Good riddance! Wish it was immediately!

Bit later, after dozing
Forced to finally go into kitchen to get a glass of water. *A* was sitting staring out the back door. I filled the glass, then asked him to get out of *my* chair. He sat down in another chair, and I stared out of the door myself. Realised I hadn't seen the kitten. Went to check on it and found it curled up on the sofa. Probably exhausted from its newfound fame. Opened the fridge, and poured the cream off the milk into a saucer, even though milk is bad for cats. Put it on the floor near the sofa. Went back to staring out the door.

Psych and the woman from PsyRo arrived half an hour late. They looked unexpectedly pleased. Psych said a brief hello. I wanted to ask why they were fetching *A*, and also if he was a snitch. But didn't.

Psych gave me the raised-eyebrow look. Say goodbye to Jeff, she said.

So I went over to where *A* had sat down again in my chair and was stroking the kitten. Goodbye, *Jeff*, I said to the back of his head. Even I could tell my face didn't look too friendly.

He turned round and gazed up at me with a calm expression. YOU HATE ME, he said, in his suave, well-modulated voice. Then he laughed. Only joking, he said, mimicking my voice perfectly. I couldn't quite read his expression. He stood up and handed me the kitten.

After they left, I fetched this *real* diary and sat staring out the back door with the kitten on my lap.

Still here. *A* is clever, after all. He's right. I do hate him. Did? Cutie, beastie, sweetie, we don't like Mother and Mother's cats, now do we? Do we?

I wonder if the kitten misses *A*?

Are You Cold, Monkey?
Are You Cold?

THE GIRL IN the puddle is not exactly dreaming ...

She lies in the water, her thoughts stacked on top of her. *Don't call it dreaming. Dreaming is nice.*

Whatever she calls it, she is wishing herself up and out of this world, she is wishing the good up and out.

On the top layer, the saucer eyes appear, spinning eyes like a monster's in a fairy tale. She wipes her hand over her face and up there is the monkey. She drifts up. The monkey looks down. Its lips crack open and show its teeth.

And the girl knows the answer: the monkey is smiling, but the monkey doesn't know what a smile is.

"Are you cold, monkey? Are you cold?" she asks.

◊

Monkey has been in a dark room since birth and it is always cold.

Monkey only knows it is cold because the girl asked the question. Up till then, he did not recognise words. The

God in the white coat took care not to talk; he wrote his thoughts into a small notebook.

When the cold and the dark started, there were no sounds except for the slapping of the girl's rubber soles in the corridor outside, the footsteps arriving with the milk and receding after the bottle was full.

It was the girl who contaminated the experiment. She whispered the question through the milk funnel when Monkey happened to be sitting in front of it; her muffled breath blew softly against his fur and heated him up.

"Warm," the girl whispered next.

Warm. Monkey felt the word caressing his face, rolling on his tongue, and he began to want warm.

◊

The Prof and the girl stand behind the one-way glass and watch the monkey. It isn't doing much. It runs from spot to spot, looking for something, distressed.

"I'll get the milk," she says.

"Remember, don't talk to it," he says.

◊

The girl sits in the lab kitchen.

On her right is an orange mug. Tomorrow she'll have her coffee in the green mug, and the next day the orange.

. . . If Mom had seen her lying in the puddle, she'd shout about the clothes and about the hair . . .

The girl's plaits are blond.

"I wish you had dark hair, like me," says her Mom.

But the girl likes her hair. It reminds her of the sun.

She imagines the monkey blond, even though she knows it is brown.

. . . If you take away the light, nothing has colour . . . What if the cups break?

This isn't dreaming. Don't call it dreaming. Dreaming is nice.

◊

The girl contaminated the experiment, but the crack had started before. It started with the white from the Prof's coat, shining out of the gloom into which Monkey was born.

Monkey saw the white coat and surmised he had been put there by God.

God was all-powerful.

God was cold like the room: his lips pulled apart, his green eyes stayed the same.

◊

The girl lies on her back in the puddle. Things drift through her: the dates of World War One and World War Two, the piece of pencil lead broken off in her brother's gum, things . . . like love, shining shadows, bruises . . . Her chest is broken bubbles . . . Water seeps in . . . up to the chin, over the mouth, up to the nose, over the nose, under forever, sleep, rest, rest forever . . .

This isn't dreaming. This isn't it. Dreaming is nice.

◊

Monkey has started seeing two large green eyes. When God is gone, they hang suspended in the room, watching everything: the lids never close.

And Monkey also notices the small white blocks that appear, shining in the dark, when God pulls up the corners of his mouth. At those times, he watches the eyes carefully. There does not seem to be a connection. Monkey taps his teeth, thinking hard, stuck.

◊

During the lunch break, when the Prof is out, the girl puts her mouth to the funnel and whispers more forbidden words. "Don't worry . . . You're normal . . . It's OK."

◊

Monkey would not recognise the girl. He has never seen her: she is always behind the glass. He has heard the footsteps and the voice, but he doesn't know what they are.

Despite everything, Monkey isn't stupid; stunted maybe, but not stupid. Monkey runs up and down, up and down, thinking . . . The light came with God, the warm, not-cold, through the funnel . . .

Monkey has not imagined the outside yet.

God is all-powerful.

God is.

Until the day the new monkey arrives.

"They won't like each other," the Prof says to the girl, as they stand behind the glass and watch.

The Prof is right. The new monkey sits in the corner and scowls. It doesn't like Monkey. And Monkey doesn't like it. He has no idea what it is.

But he has seen God and his white coat, he has heard and felt 'warm', and now there is a clue . . . Something about the height: God is high above, but the new monkey locks eyes with him. Then there is the tail – he has one, it has one – and the toes and the paws and the fur, they are the same.

What remains is the face. Monkey runs his hand over his face from top to bottom, as if he is opening something out, or closing something down. He tap, tap, taps his teeth.

Monkey had only seen one pair of eyes, one mouth, before he met the new monkey. He would like very much to put out his paw and move it down its face, slide off the dream. He is beginning to suspect something . . .

Monkey would like to, but he is afraid. The new monkey does not pull up the corners of its mouth. Its brown eyes bore into Monkey.

◊

The girl watches the monkeys, her hand covering her lips, her head against the glass.

. . . Mom sprayed antifreeze into my mouth this morning so I could act like a normal girl, a temporary girl. I walked out the house in a straight line and lay down in a puddle.

She checks the corridor in both directions, then whispers into the funnel:

"This isn't dreaming. Dreaming is nice."

◊

When the Prof brings in the cloth and wire mothers, Monkey isn't sure what to do. Something enters he can't touch or begin to understand, something strumming softly on the back of his brain: the crack started by the white coat, the warm, the other monkey . . . He feels the wedge go in deeper and the gap widens.

The cloth mother and the wire mother have odd faces; they don't look like the new monkey.

Monkey feels a heaving in the chest, a wish, a want for something he did not know was missing.

He touches his face, then points to the new monkey's face.

It rubs its face and points back.

Monkey feels his lips cracking apart, pulled up by some unknown force, and his teeth showing, like God's. The new monkey does the same. And Monkey feels warm. In the dark, their grins widen, even though they have no idea what a grin is.

◊

The girl watches from behind the glass. She can see how it hurts those monkeys to smile, how the Prof has forced them to smile. The thing is, if she was Monkey, she wouldn't want the cloth monkey, or the wire monkey, or the new monkey. She wouldn't want any of them. She just wants to lie in a puddle. That is what she wants.

◊

The monkeys begin to play. They make forays to the wire apparition, daring, outdoing each other. They run close and shriek in terror. And grin in relief when they get back to the opposite side of the room.

◊

Behind the one-way glass, the Prof and the girl watch.

Not liking the way things are going, those cooperative monkey grins, the Prof turns on the thermostat, pumping warmth into the cloth mother.

◊

Monkey touches the cloth first. It gives. It is warm. He hesitates, then reaches out his arms and nestles his head in the cloth.

The new monkey stares. It runs up and pokes in a finger. It tries to pull Monkey off. Monkey turns round and bites it hard.

Monkey spends the night on the cloth mother, watching the new monkey out of the corner of his eye. It edges closer to the wire mother, then jabs out a finger and recoils in horror; down its face goes wet.

Buried in his cloth, Monkey feels a stab of difference.

◊

The monkeys brood in the dark. There is only one cloth

mother, only room for one on its chest. They scream and fight, taking turns on the cloth, turns at defeat.

They could cling together, but their eyes glitter against each other.

◊

The girl covers her ears to block out the monkeys' screeching and carries on bringing the milk.

What more is the Prof going to find? For God's sake, even I know what is wrong with those monkeys.

"Stop it! You are the same," she shouts into the funnel, not caring if the Prof can hear.

◊

It becomes unbearable; she goes outside and lies on the grass, looking up into the trees, wishing . . .

She knows that at least one monkey will escape. She knows because she is going to help it out of its dark room into the light. She will use a blindfold at first. And when she finally uncovers its massive monkey eyes, it will see patterns, kaleidoscopes of greens, yellows, blues, and reds. Gradually things will take shape: trees, grass, the stream at the bottom of the meadow.

This is dreaming. This is it! Dreaming is nice.

But at the moment the world sears in, the monkey will bury its face in her coat, it will desperately cling, it will be blind.

She will face away from the lab. She will put her arms around it, its furry back pressed against her, and gently direct its gaze outwards; little by little, warmth will seep in and it will see.

◊

When the Prof returns from lunch, the room is empty. His green eyes scan the gloom. No, it is not empty: one small monkey clings to the cloth mother. He recognises it as the new monkey from the silver patch on its shoulder. "Where's your friend and foe, hey?" he asks in a soft voice.

But he knows the answer already; he has noticed the way the girl looks at those monkeys – and at him. And he is strangely pleased.

"Poor bastard monkey." He sighs. "If you could understand what we are searching for. If you only knew what you are doing on her behalf."

The monkey turns its head and watches the Prof's lips pulling up to show his teeth.

◊

Monkey's eyes burn as he clings to the inside of the girl's coat; he is screaming for the cloth mother, he is screaming for the new monkey, he is screaming with joy and with fear at the light. All this light.

Dividual

1. The Doctor's Notes

Sometimes we have to chop the patients' hands off (it's a case of survival) to convince them that, yes, this is real, this is happening, this physical body is you, is yours.

"We'll grow them back," we reassure them, but even this doesn't usually get much of a reaction. (Or, if it does, all they want to know is whether the new hands can grow back different to how they look now.)

They sit and stare at the bandaged stumps, but they don't see them.

Sometimes they mutter and glance wildly around the room in what we now know is a search for a mirror. Sometimes I find my eyes following theirs – empathic mirroring. To be encouraged in most circumstances. I force my gaze into a fixed position in front of these patients.

At the very least, the stumps prevent the patients taking photos. To add to the complexity of the illness, we know it isn't the mirror alone; it is the photos taken in the mirror. Even imagining a photo being taken leads to subtle shifts in how they present themselves.

Exasperated, we may eventually say something like: "It doesn't matter what you look like."

"I already know what I look like," is a typical reply.

Invariably, the self that is described by the patient (in rare moments of lucidity) bears little physical resemblance to the self seen in a mirror.

The hand-chopping was preceded by an experiment in which the eyes were (temporarily) removed. At first, of course, we used a blindfold, but people cheated and pulled it off when our backs were turned.

The experiment failed. It was too quick and too frightening for the patients. They had no experience of consciousness without sight. This, we are slowly realising, takes much practice and they hadn't been trained. Rather than let go, they clung more than ever to 'the true selfie', something they created from a mash-up of famous people (a lot of them about): singers, models, whoever they wanted.

It seems obvious now that would happen.

Those few of us doctors left who have an orientation to the real world know it is a race against time because how long before we, the new minority, succumb to the illness all around us? We cling to objective reality (what else can we do?) to counteract the non-responses of the subjects, now making up most of the world. It is a precarious position, but we must keep the fire of the exterior world alive because otherwise the subjects will cease to engage with material conditions, including other people, and, eventually, society will end.

On the plus side, we work in conditions of unprecedented freedom; it is unlikely that the patients will stop us. In comparison to current social relations, the alienation of late capitalism feels like a warm and welcoming dream of brotherhood, to be wished for with much nostalgia by those of us left guarding the outside of things.

It is a race against time and a race against ourselves.

In extreme cases, which are most cases these days, we prescribe, as a matter of urgency, a trek to the interior.

The trek begins with a mirror. Counter-intuitive, you'd think; after all, the whole thing started with mirrors. The technique comes from homeopathy (long discredited but useful in psychology as a working metaphor): treatment with a tiny dose of the poison that caused the symptoms in the first place.

In these cases, this means that the patient must look into a mirror (briefly) to start the search for the true self that, gazed at too long, hardens into something else. 'Be whoever you want to be' proved to be a fantasy of self that outdazzles the more accurate measure of reflected-back human consensus (imperfect, but somehow necessary). We are belatedly realising that no man is an island, etc.

Let's face it, it is an inexact and mostly untested science. Us doctors don't know whether the one we hope to bring back will be the real self.

2. The Patient's Story

Yes, I admit it. I admit it happened to me too. Why else am I telling you this story?

Once I was better, the doctors told me they'd discovered the cure by accident during a study on a spike in the time prisoners were spending in solitary confinement.

Solitary didn't work any more. Instead of acting as a deterrent, all of the prisoners wanted to try it. The doctors think it was because the brain was tired of drugs and alcohol and films and games, all the usual entertainment. The prisoners were so bored and so far away from interior stuff that going inside themselves was a harsh thrill. A dark dare. "The sooooul," they said, laughing to themselves, attacking each other just to get thrown in the cooler.

Yes, I admit I was a prisoner. A minor crime against F—— b——, in case you're asking. They kept switching my profile pics without permission, giving the wrong impression of me.

I know I needed some excitement. I was one of the first test subjects. The doctors tricked me. But I understand I had to think it was my idea to go in. I understand I had to be bored enough to stay in the interior for a while. For a long time, nobody guessed the doctors were behind it. They thought it was their own, rebel selfies.

2.1 This is what is supposed to happen

I now know that it was the doctors who arranged for a 'cleaner' to casually drop a small, plastic-backed hand mirror under my cell bed. They also arranged for the 'cleaner' to come back into the room exactly two seconds after I found it. It's important not to look into the mirror for too long.

I would tell you what I saw, but the doctors discourage remembering what they call 'the fixed selfie'. Common people call it 'the one true selfie'.

The glance into the mirror is followed by a wagon. There are always wagons, old-fashioned, white canvas pulled taut over hoops, covered in blood from dead settlers who set off to steal land. These days, the indigenous people have guns and they know how to shoot accurately from a good distance.

Once you have chosen your wagon – they all look the same – you begin the trek.

As you leave, people are making huge fires with words, with pictures and words, and also just with pictures. Nobody is taking photos. Nobody wants to take photos. The two-storey-high, neon F——b—— v103 logo lies on its side. The crowd takes an axe to it, and you watch the smiling selfies go up in flames, along with their 'likes'. Nobody wants to be friends anymore – the crowd burns the oversharers first, with their sad holiday snaps and their personality types and food. Their frozen selfies. The doctors told me that nobody ever found themselves this way.

The journey ahead is long and the sky flames behind you.

You leave a lot behind, but it feels like nothing. All those years staring at stuff and it takes a second for none of it to matter. You walk away from the blazing letters, emptied, the old world gone as you crunch across the shells of burnt-out phones.

On this journey, you are alone.

Occasionally, as you lead your horses through the carnage, you brush up against another leaver and physical touch feels strange. You feel a twinge of envy for the people on the outside, but this disappears from your mind when you see the faces around you, when you are forced to rub up raw. Faces with open pores and furrowed brows. The kind of faces that you secretly knew others had, that you had. What was all that competing about, you ask yourself.

You must sweat and heave, you must push yourself

beyond what you can endure, until you have shown yourself worthy. I forget of what.

If you are bored already, if that happens, you must trek for another few weeks until you have forgotten altogether what you look like. The wagons have no mirrors and anything shiny, such as a gleaming spoon polished on an apron, is forbidden.

This is as real as it gets these days, say the doctors.

That moment the doctors call the 'solo sado-erotic power delusion' stays in your memory: standing on some ridge looking down and imagining that you possess the territory, not realising that things are literally about to go downhill.

At last, when you reach the limits of your endurance, when everything is burnt and gone and you are lying, bleeding, face down next to your wagon, regretting your ignorance and stupidity, your sorry wish for power and domination, you look up.

Surrounded by dead settlers, you are the only one left, but you don't feel brave, you don't feel like conquering, you don't really even feel like being a rugged individual.

A flash of light, bright against the yellow grass, catches your eye. Curious, you crawl over to it. A mirror is propped incongruously against the broken axle of the wagon. You look into it and you see:

A strange, ugly human face, water cutting grooves through make-up and blood and dirt.

Tears? you think, amazed.

You gaze at the face, fascinated as the tears fall more thickly. You catch your breath. It is, You.

You lie belly down in the dry grass and watch this

person, this You. You watch for quite a while, until you smile into the mirror, then turn away of your own accord.

You are inside already, but another inside appears, an inside of thoughts and painful contemplation. It goes something like this:

I struggle through my days, through my life, and things keep going wrong. I keep going wrong. I keep deviating from myself, from the true me. I glimpse it, but then it hides. Why should I listen to the true self? Try to understand it? Why does it insist on staying trapped inside? Is it even real? If it's so fucking authentic, then why doesn't it just fucking come out?

This goes on for as long as it needs to.

"Who am I?" you finally shout.

The true selfie shatters and the real self breaks through.

2.2 This is what sometimes happens – this is what happened to me

At last, you reach the limits of your endurance, regretting your ignorance and stupidity, your sorry wish for power. You look around at the bleeding bodies, you look into the mirror propped up on the axle.

Stupid, stupid, you think. You have let yourself down. Why go on the trek if you are going to cry? Pathetic!

A dialogue starts inside:

Today I am my grumpy self, my obstinate self, the self that got left out in the cold and has never forgotten or forgiven, the self who hates the real me. What if I'm not kind? Or humble? Or a fighter? What if this self grew in secret until it took over the whole world, the world of me? What if you covered your mouth with your hand and you said "That isn't you"? And

*what if I replied that it wasn't? It wasn't me. What if I am
not a nice person?*

You collapse in tears. "Where are these dumb-fuck
doctors taking me?" you scream. "What are they doing
to me?"

I fell apart, as the doctors say, although I prefer the
old-fashioned term 'nervous breakdown'. It sounds much
more glamorous (than feeling like you do not wish to exist
because it is fucking unbearable and you do not wish to die
because that too is fucking unbearable).

It was like something had taken me over. I, or part
thereof, had taken me over.

I looked in the mirror too much. I took photos. That's
what started it.

So they took me to the hospital and they rested me
for a while. After my trek, I lay in bed for quite some
time and contemplated things such as: do I belong to this
world, to these people who can no longer stand still and
sing together, who can't even smile at each other?

Hard to know who I was.

I could have been anybody.

One day, I thought from my hospital bed, I will sit with
all of my other selves around a campfire and converse. Will
they recognise me? I don't know, but I will sit and watch
them, the real me will watch them, and I'm sure that each
of them will be watching me back, admiringly, wishing
they had a true self (wishing that they were me).

Now, when I glance in the mirror, I'm a perfect stranger.

I always wanted to be a doctor. And here I am.

Grow Your Gorilla

THE FOREST FLOOR behind my old house is velvet soft, the dark fingers of trees clutching each other in the wind. A thousand pairs of bright yellow eyes stare at me from the branches – like that gorilla in the zoo – as if they love me, as if they would like to kill me.

I know they aren't alive. Still, I feel their breath against my face as I pass. It's just the wind, I tell myself, but I sense reproach. Are your bones more real than plastic? they seem to whisper.

I lean against a trunk, pretending not to be scared, and stare back, their eyes stirring something in me.

The wind changes to clicks and whirrs, stunted hands beating on small chests. I can't turn off a thousand switches; I must get out.

I have to find you first.

◊

You came from the forest. OK, I opened you on Christmas day, but I knew it was the hair I'd planted. I waited impatiently for my presents on Christmas morning. And mine from Mum, I knew, I hoped, was a gorilla. Most of my friends already had one, but that's not why I wanted you – I was too old by then to play with toys. I knew I could make you come alive, I knew you would be the true one.

I went into the woods at the bottom of my garden – there were no broken gorillas hanging from the branches then. I brought a stolen hair, plucked from a friend's gorilla, and I put it under a tree in a bowl of water and I prayed.

When I saw the tiny box in my Christmas stocking, I knew what it was.

The gorilla came from China.

"Another piece of plastic shit," Dad said, frowning at Mum as I opened the box. "Fifty percent of China's emissions come from the crap we buy from them."

True, because you were just a plastic pod then. But I wanted you. I wanted you and I wished I'd never shown Dad. I hid the packaging from him when I saw how big you might – you would – become.

"Grow your Gorilla," said the instructions. Each gorilla had the potential to grow, they explained, but only one would grow into a true gorilla. I knew it would be you.

Grow. Grow. Grow.

Of course, I had the odd doubt. What if you were like one of those sea monkeys advertised on the back of comics? My friend told me they were just water fleas.

But you looked like a real gorilla, with your eyes, nose, your little teeth, and perfect ears flattened back against your head. They pressed the fingers out individually to make them more lifelike, your serial number on your thumb, to be erased and replaced by unique fingerprints if a certain height was reached.

You stood in the middle of my palm in all of your potential silverback glory, and I could already see myself crying into your fur as I released you on some mountain top. I planned to let you go from the beginning, after you'd grown twice the size, three times, no, twenty times at least, big, with a silver strip of fur across your back. You would be mine, and then I would let you go.

I thanked Mum and sat quietly and read the instructions:

1. Turn power switch to on.

2. Please, put the gorilla in a damp place. A forest is perfect, or a windowsill with a saucer of water.

3. Please, pour on its head a little vegetable oil, a little water, depending on the type of gorilla you think it will be.

4. Water three times a day.

5. If handled good, it will grow. How much is up to you. (There is only one true gorilla, to be found by the lucky, but, more important, the right person!!)

6. If the gorilla doesn't grow, or if stunted, buy a new one, start again. (Special discount for second-time buyers.)

7. Merry Christmas!

On Christmas night, after my parents had gone to bed, I took you out of your pod for the first time and put you on the windowsill. I overwatered you; your tiny coat was ruffled and damp. I hung you from the radiator to dry. Your eyes hadn't opened yet. But I didn't switch you on. I couldn't bear to. I was waiting for you to come alive by yourself.

Every day after school, as the winter dusk fell, I pedalled past the windows stretched along my street, two sad yellow eyes in each looking outwards at the rising moon and waiting for the miracle. They all came from the same factory, but only one belonged in the forest. They were already different sizes. I imagined the silver hairs starting to prick through the backs of some of them – the sign of the mature male – and I was tempted to switch you on.

After that Christmas, when the gorillas began to grow, they sold at a furious rate. Even adults were obsessed. They bought more and more until it became a frenzy: they all wanted the true one. Of course, I didn't tell them that I already had you. News articles compared the relative size of the gorillas and discussed the genetics of the silver hair. There was even speculation about secret experiments.

It lasted until the end of January. Reports confirmed that no gorilla had grown more than three times its size. The manufacturers refused interviews and the factory closed down shortly afterwards.

People were furious when they couldn't get their money back. The news ran a story about a woman travelling to the edge of a forest.

"Get back in the trees!" she screamed, as she flung her stunted gorilla into the branches, and soon people all over the world were doing the same.

"Jesus!" said Dad. "Why aren't they recycling them at least?"

I was relieved when he didn't ask about you. I took you out of my window, which faced the street, and sat you overlooking the back garden and the woods with its dark trees. You were still switched off and had not grown at all. I opened your yellow eyes myself. You looked sad and reproachful as we watched the kids at the bottom of my garden flinging their gorillas into the trees. I wondered what you were thinking. I wondered if you thought at all.

Mid-February, I took you to the woods and we peered in together. The eyes of the gorillas glowed yellow and sad. Their faces and backs were broken, their beautiful hands ripped off, wires dangling from branches. A low whirring sound, almost a grunt, mixed in with the wind blowing through the trees.

"Don't ever drop your gorilla," it said on the warning labels in large red letters, but people threw them anyway.

There were reports about strange screams and howls, batteries that wouldn't run down. Some even claimed to have seen the big one, usually teenage boys who dared each other into the forests that most people were too scared to enter.

I gave in and switched you on at the end of February.

You only grew while I slept; when I stayed awake to watch you, nothing happened. I measured you each morning: your growth was almost imperceptible – a three millimetre average, maybe five millimetres or so on a good night – but you were slowly getting bigger. Just as well, I thought. If you grew too fast then Mum and Dad would notice.

I still believed you were the one.

You doubled in height before you stopped. For weeks after, I measured you each morning, but you hadn't grown.

Dad came into my bedroom one evening and saw you slumped against the wall. "I can take it down to the recycling. I'm going on Sunday," he said.

I didn't reply.

I'd planned to hide you in the woods until Dad's recycling trip was over. I was going to build you a little shelter, keep watering you each day.

When you left, you were still only twice your original size. You weren't big enough to be without me. I came home from school and you were gone. I asked Dad if he'd seen you. I was convinced he'd thrown you away, until I saw the tiny footprints leading out the back door.

"Bloody wet moggy again," said Dad, grabbing the mop.

I followed the footprints through the kitchen and out onto the back lawn, where they faded into the grass. I went to the bottom of the garden and called to you for hours, but all I could hear was the wind in the trees.

I thought about you alone in the dark and gloom, I thought about going after you for weeks. But by the time I'd worked up the nerve, I'd decided that you wouldn't grow big after all. You were just like all the others. Dad must have taken you. And if he hadn't, I would have flung you into the trees myself. Dad was, as always, right: of course it was just the cat.

◊

I've completely forgotten about you by the time I'm at college. Mum and Dad move house. They ask me to pick up the last few boxes on my way to visit them over the Christmas holidays.

The house is empty for a few months before the new owners move in and I pack the boxes into the van quickly. I'm locking the back door when I hear a howl coming from the woods. I can't help thinking of those little footprints, of you.

They'd proved long ago that there was no true gorilla, but I find myself walking down to the trees. It's probably a dog, or maybe a wounded animal.

I stand on the threshold and stare at the yellow eyes lighting faint paths through the undergrowth. It's just switches and cheap genetics, I tell myself, but even with special batteries, it seems impossible that they can still be working – it's been at least four years.

There is no true gorilla.

But if these gorillas are still switched on, then you . . . Are your eyes still gleaming in the dark? Are you still so small?

I am washed through with shame and longing. I abandoned you.

I race into the trees, pushing through the branches hung with failed silverbacks, their yellow eyes staring, their mournful barks filling the cold air.

Deep in the woods, I slump against a tree, looking for your yellow eyes. But there are so many gorillas. I hang my head.

I smell you before I see you, a pungent, musky smell. I lift my head and listen to the sound of your big feet landing on the soft pine needles. I wait.

The yellow eyes all turn to you as you enter the clearing.

Your steps seem mechanical before I realise that you are moving naturally, as would a real, wounded gorilla. You have a slight limp in your right front paw. You are magnificent, true gorilla size with a strip of silver fur across your back.

You don't see me at first. You reach up to a branch and gently remove the remains of a pod from a half-opened gorilla, with your big thick sensitive fingers. The tiny gorilla emerges silky and smooth, like you did when I first opened you. You switch it on and set it gently on the ground before rescuing another, then another.

I am full of the thoughts of wounded gorillas. And there were thousands made, millions perhaps. I have betrayed the whole world. I cannot stifle my sobbing.

You turn towards me and rise up on your hind legs.

I am so small, but I hold out my hands in hallelujah, I hold up my face, ready to be smashed. I wait, trembling. I wait for you.

You come right up to me and put your face close to mine. You stare into my eyes. I notice that yours have deepened to dark brown.

You press my chest with your wounded, leathery hand.

I curl my fingers into yours. Slowly, I feel your warmth transfuse into my body. You know me.

I watch as you gather more gorillas from the trees and stand them on the ground. Only one was supposed to make it, but now a whole troop is coming to life under the frosty moon, eyes glinting off the trunks of the pines.

You look at me one last time, before you turn to the troop.

You beat your chest and they follow after you, deeper

into the woods. I watch your silver threading into the darkness. I imagine plastic being spun into fur; I imagine forests that only the true and the brave can enter.

I drive to my parents' new house and unload the boxes.

"How was the old house?" asks Dad, over lunch.

I want to tell Dad all about it, about the silver fur that I can still see from the corner of my eye, but all I say is "I bet at least some of those gorillas were recycled."

And Dad smiles.

The Edges of Seasons

THE WAKING SHOULD be clean and swift, a rush of ice to sky.

◊

Now it's warmer, the swans forget to migrate. They stay and stay and suddenly it's cold and it's too late to go anywhere else, so they bob in the small patch of water on the edge of the ice, the only things moving against the white crackling trees, and the mercury is dropping: minus seven, minus eight.

◊

A girl walked onto the ice . . .

◊

"Don't go on the lake in winter," the mother said. "The drowned girl will get you."

"But where is she in summer?" the girl asked.

"Changed into a swan and flown away," said the mother. "Gone south to warm her bones."

◊

Warm orange lines of traffic flow along the far side of the lake as I walk to work. A swan cries out into the stiff dark sky. It sits in the middle of the frozen water, its blurred wings beating between daylight and darkness. It sounds distressed.

I look at my watch. I look at the ice. I can just make out the outlines of dirty weeds underneath. I reach down and pick up a stone. I throw it onto the surface. It makes a hard, hollow sound as it bounces.

◊

"In the winter," said the mother, "the girl sleeps under the ice in her coffin of darkness. In summer, she'll rise in the form of a swan and fly south, to her country."

◊

This winter, these last winters, as a concerned mother might say, it is too warm under the ice. The girl's rest is over. Before, she lived in cold slumber and joyful swift waking to flight. Now she sleeps fitfully, her skin red and chafing where feathers bud and then retract and disappear. Her sleep is broken with dreams of flying. She shivers for the first time in the icy water, where the edges of the seasons merge for too long.

◊

The sky is lightening. The swan beats its wings harder and I can see that it is trying to fly, but it's trapped in the ice.

This is not the weather for swans.

I have no feeling for these snake-necked creatures. I've always been scared of them. I pass their winter quarters every morning on my way to work, in my adopted country where I have never felt completely at home.

They shouldn't be here. But they don't even try to fly. They just waddle across the path on their big, ungainly feet, scaring tourists and small children.

Whatever happened to instinct?

◊

"The girl is not used to opening her eyes under the water," said the mother. The ice sheet over her face thins and thickens according to the erratic weather. She lies looking up at the distorted sky, a darker blue when seen through ice. At noon, she turns her head when the light shafts straight into her eyes, like knives or upside-down spires. At other times, the sun slants shyly in and she daydreams of cathedrals of leaves, seen from above. And she dreams of flying south, warm sun melting the film of ice on her back.

◊

The swan cries out. The first time I have heard a swan cry like that, and I have lived here a long time, almost all my life.

Have compassion for all creatures, a mother might say. Fly away, fly away home, a mother might also say.

◊

On my first school hike after I arrived, we got caught in a white-out in minus thirty. I couldn't tell up from down, I couldn't measure anything at all. The drop to my left looked twenty metres deep and I leapt away, but it was only two.

How they laughed at me later when we were sitting inside next to a raging fire. "At least we can see *you* in the snow," they joked, although most of my face had been covered.

Then they told stories where things always worked out well, the way they had come to expect.

◊

A woman walks onto the ice . . .

◊

Is the ice strong enough to hold my weight? Never, a concerned mother would say. I use a frosty branch for support and inch my way onto the lake. My foot slides out from under me and I nearly fall.

I'm back on shore and the swan's cries are louder as the sky brightens to a dull grey.

Light.

I look at my watch.

My dad once told me a story about a brave man who stripped down to his pants to rescue a dog trapped in the ice. It bit him and then ran away, but he saved it. I never asked: why did he take off his clothes?

I return to my house and fill a bucket with hot water. On my way back to the lake, I avoid thinking about the girl under the ice.

I strip down to my long johns and jumper and woollen socks. No point in going all the way. I don't want my skin to stick. I put the bucket down on the ice and crouch behind it. The man's stripping makes sense now: less weight. I should have taken off my jumper, but I'm glad for the warmth. I lie face down and spread out my body: distributed weight.

A flurry of snow dusts the surface and I'm grateful. I don't want to see the girl's face staring up at me. It was only a mother's tale, but . . .

I push the bucket in front of me and use my elbows to propel myself forward.

It's hard work and I'm thirsty. I resist the urge to lick the ice. I know rationally it would not be a good idea. I know my tongue would stick.

I crane around and look back at the icy trees in the distance. I rest my head on my arms and squint sideways at the swan. It looks different from this angle: Majestic and enormous. Terrifying.

I push forward until I'm a few metres away from it. It stretches its neck towards me and hisses.

Behind me, I can hear shouts.

My body is shivering involuntarily, like a bird without feathers.

If I don't help it, it will die. I slide closer, skimming my hands, the bucket in front of my face to protect me from being pecked.

The swan flaps its wings, looming above me, hurting itself.

Its hard beak strikes my hands on the other side of the bucket. I cry out and yet I leave them there; I feel as if something in this situation is my fault.

The swan's neck droops over its torn feathers. Seams of red spread through its whiteness. As if the thin lines are ready to split it apart.

I need to get closer.

I am right next to it when it lifts its head and jabs me hard in my side. Hot water slops onto the ice and scalds my fingers.

I feel warmth as I watch the red seeping through my jumper.

"We are all the same inside," Dad used to say when I told him what they'd called me at school, rubbing his blond head against my dark one.

The bucket is heavy. I struggle to tip it. Finally, I manage to shove it over and the hot water flows onto the ice around the swan. It makes its own little pool in the hardness. I spread the water with my wet gloves, dissolving the dusting of snow.

The swan shrieks and strains while tears freeze on my cheeks, and I can't stop watching. I can almost hear its feathers tearing.

The ice starts to crack.

I swivel round, but the cracks radiate out from me. For a moment, I am the centre of the lake, the centre of the ice.

I never asked Dad: Why did the dog run away? Why did Mum run away?

A great hand is tilting the world, the water and the trees sliding south down the map. But the swan and I stay stuck in the north because the north is too warm, but not warm enough sometimes.

◊

A girl walked onto the ice a long time ago . . .

She kept walking until she was dead centre. She lay on her back and spread out her arms. She counted the stars as the ice froze to her body, then melted underneath her, as she slowly sank into the dark water of the lake.

"She thought she would have to stay forever," the mother said. "But then she became a swan."

◊

I can't remember the south, but I've seen the pictures of my mum as a girl. For a long time, I wanted to go home, to her country. I cried when my friends rolled up their trousers and bared their pink knees to sunbathe in the snow. All I could do was shiver.

◊

My last dream is not about me. I look up as the ice above my face explodes into white wings beating against the sky. How I envy the swan flying south. Perhaps it will finally find somewhere to stay warm.

Pain Is a Liar

*I*N THE DARK *forest, there is fear. But the fear is really in the sun glaring above you, in the gaze of the others around you.*

"Remember the old days, when it used to hurt?" they tease him.

"Not really," Anton answers the coterie, forgetting about the voice, and he stretches his ankles out a little on the bed, hoping that the stretch is imperceptible.

But they are distracted, talking among themselves, and it is very gloomy, and he finally dares to let his eyes dart sideways to the windows that go all the way down to the floor. The wind is blowing the cherry blossoms hard against the panes. In the deepening dusk, they have a quality of something. Something important. He can't explain it. And does it even matter?

Yes, says the voice, *it matters.*

He pretends the coterie's incessant whispering is the wind outside. He imagines each splotch of blossom driving one of them from the room.

They finally say they are going for ice creams or a beer or something, but they don't invite him.

In any case, he doesn't like ice cream, not after some-body else has licked it, anyway.

He is left alone with impressions of soft pink smash-ing against glass. It's not quite enough to stop him shiver-ing. He makes hard fists, careful not to leave any marks. He keeps his fingernails short. They are not the least bit interested in how he looks, as long as he doesn't hurt himself.

"The experiments are voluntary," they tell him.

He lifts his head and studies his toes. All there. But they are bent, broken.

"Pain is only in the brain," they say. "Use your brain to control your pain."

So why doesn't he just get up and go?

Pain is a liar, pain is in the brain, he thinks. He slides his leg up the bed. "Holy little fucking gods, it hurts!" he shouts at the trees.

They've left painkillers, but if he takes them they'll think he's weak.

He imagines arms closing round him, the arms of a long-dead father. *Shush, little monkey, shush*, the imaginary father says.

And then he is part of the darkness.

◊

He wakes and calls Jen, one of the remaining members of his herd, to come and pick him up. He knows it's over for today, that they won't return. Of course, they are much cleverer than him and hard to predict, but they are easily distracted.

Jen bustles in. "Anton," she says, and she smiles at him in a way that makes him feel he's weak.

But this is precisely why he called her: she spends a lot of time in the gym and is strong enough to support him to a car.

She probably assumes he's taken the painkillers, but he's hidden them in his undershirt pocket. His imagination is not strong enough to dull the pain and he'll need them for later.

He wants to ask her if she's ever done such tests, but he can't bring himself to. If she has, he bets she wouldn't have used painkillers.

"Come on, you big bub," she says, placing her arm around his back and helping him to sit up sideways on the bed.

He squeezes his eyes closed for a moment. He opens them and looks down at his toes dangling like twisted roots.

He bites his lip.

She hoists him onto his feet. The strength of his scream surprises them both.

She lays him back down and digs in a pocket. "I was saving it for later, but you better—"

She pushes the painkiller into his mouth. For a moment, before he passes out, he feels as if she could be the arms.

◊

I have been in the gaps of your sleepless hours.

Anton wakes to the voice. But there is no one there. He lies on the bed in his little attic room, staring at the curve of yellow moon, bright against the dark square of window. Jen's pill has almost worn off and the pain is seeping back. He is contemplating taking the hidden painkillers, when the coterie comes in without knocking. They stand around his bed, staring down at him like excited children.

He can see they have been shopping: they are barefoot, with crowns of thorns and torn white loincloths, splotches of red deliberately staining the finely woven fabric.

They are dressed like their fashionable little god, Jesus Christ. The one who hung and suffered there. "For all of us," they say, and giggle. "Except for you."

And Pocock bends and wiggles Anton's big toe.

He can't help grimacing.

Sometimes this expression makes them happy and they stop. But he tries not to grimace again. Sometimes they don't like the fact that he is more like Jesus than them, that he can suffer.

He wishes he were a lot more like Jesus. Why is his pain threshold so low?

Shush, little monkey, shush, they'll get bored.

"Pain is a liar," he says with a controlled wince, and they are satisfied. Thank their little god!

He stares at their beautiful faces and wishes they could feel pain, that he could watch their faces contort in agony.

Don't be mean, Anton, he tells himself. It isn't their fault.

The moon wavers in front of Anton's eyes. Pain is a liar. Pain is a liar.

They leave soon after, to go sightseeing or something.

Ha! He's fooled them. They've left him alone because they think he's taken the pills. He's no fun.

But their lack of interest bothers him. He knows they

are right: he's weak. His hand reaches into his pocket, and he finally swallows their pills. They work fast and he sits up and wrenches his toes back into place one by one. He is quite expert now. He has done this before.

He wishes he had the coterie's stoicism in the face of pain. But it's like beauty, he tells himself. They were born that way.

He remembers the blossoms smashing against the panes. Thank their little Jesus they forget about the herd sometimes. Despite being so clever, they think that the members of the herd are all alike. They would never call themselves a herd. They are individuals.

In the dark forest, there is fear, but the fear is really . . .

Shadows of cool leaves swim in his head; soft moonlight ripples over his aching body, soothing him with gentle stripes of light and dark.

He feels as if he has been in this house forever. Long ago, there were some happy days among the herd, until the coterie started to take a special interest in him.

"He's so sensitive, he feels everything," Pocock used to say, stroking his head, giving him treats. Before the tests started.

Now the herd is thinning. Some of them just disappeared.

"Gone to pasture," the coterie told him, when he asked. And they laughed. As usual. They find a lot of things funny.

And Dad? Was there a Dad? He can't really be the strange voice, can he?

Either way, he'll never tell them about it. If they knew, they'd notice him for longer. Hopefully, they will soon get bored. If he can just manage to work out what they want.

He often wishes they would put him out to pasture, wherever that is. But he has to make them happy first. And he wants to please them, he does. It's just that he wishes he knew more tricks, stuff that didn't hurt so much.

◊

It's the fingers again this week. He might have known. He understands that they need to do the tests, but why the fingers, why the toes? Why not his back or his stomach? Somewhere else so that he can still walk and pick things up, as well as keep them happy.

They tell him it's important. And voluntary. But if there's yet another round after this one, they'll have to rejuvenate his tissue. They promised him that they would. And they will, won't they?

They start with the bending back and the pain scale of one to ten. He can see the determined look in Pocock's eyes.

"We have to establish an objective measure of pain," Pocock says, "before we can realistically assess its extent."

Pocock is the most rational. He picks up a hammer, and before anyone can stop him, seizes Anton's wrist and brings it down hard on his finger.

"Was that a ten?" asks Pocock.

Anton's face is white with not screaming.

"Oh, Pocock, why do you always have to be so extreme?" says Marj, the smallest of the group. "Why do you always have to break everything so quickly?"

They have not blocked their ears. Your cry simply passes them by; they cannot hear it.

He doesn't know where he is. He runs towards the voice. He runs towards the arms. Dad? Dad?

He comes round, feeling sad and alone. What if the voice is like the pain: only in his head?

The coterie is still there. He holds up a damaged hand; he dares to signal that he can't do more today. And they grumble, but they are smiling.

"Pocock, you ass," says Tarquin, but he is smiling too.

Pocock gives Anton the painkillers, without him even asking. "Well done, you," he says, and Anton can't help feeling pleased. It's the first time Pocock has praised him.

Pocock smiles down at him. Pocock looks young, like him, but it's impossible to tell – they all look young. "Later, write down what you feel," Pocock says, passing him a digital pad. "Write down how much pain you feel, on a scale of one to ten."

Anton nods, woozy.

He sleeps after they leave and wakes up still in bliss, his head fuzzy. But he has to do it now, before the pills wear off. Only one finger today. He sucks in his breath and pulls it straight. No pain, but he doesn't like the click.

The pad is lying next to him on the bed. He notices something has been typed.

Why? Why try and try and try? Why be? Why me?

He stares and stares. He feels uneasy. Did Pocock write it? A practical joke? Or was it the voice?

Either way, they better not find it. But why does he care? It is all voluntary. He can do whatever he likes.

The pills are wearing off. He limps next door to

Jen's. She has a bigger attic room than his, with a private entrance.

He can't decide whether to tell her about the voice and they sit in silence for a while. In the end, he holds out his hand to show her his fingers. It doesn't hurt that much yet, he thinks, so why do I want to cry?

"You've got to get through. If you show too much pain, they'll carry on," she says, and then he can't stop the tears.

He's worried she'll be disgusted by his weakness. But she reaches under her mattress, then hands him a pill. He has a strange longing to throw his arms around her. He swallows the pill instead.

"They have everything," he says. "Why do they need me?"

"It's a sort of retro thing for them," says Jen.

He doesn't understand, but the pill works fast and soon he doesn't care.

"I've only got a few pills left," she says. "You have got to try harder."

◊

The coterie has gone on a trip. He has the house to himself for a few days. Time for his fingers to heal, although they haven't left any painkillers.

The house records everything except the attic, but they don't usually bother to watch the recordings. They have new things they'd rather do.

In any case, they know they can trust him not to run away, they know how loyal he is. And, after all, it's voluntary.

Nonetheless, he can't sleep and the voice is getting louder in the night. He lies on his bed, trying to overcome the pain. "Pain is in the brain. Pain is a liar. Fear is a liar," he mutters.

But he's weak and the pain persists. He worries that it will get even worse. He's not good enough for the coterie. He can't make them happy. He can't work out what they want. They need someone stronger, someone like Jen.

His fingers and toes are lumpy. They will make them better after they've finished the tests. They will, won't they?

When he first came to the house, they used to fuss over him a bit, in their own way. He misses their little pats, their treats, their admiring laughs. He has a strange longing for the past. A side effect of the memory erasures, he supposes. The coterie is always telling him that he is full of side effects, that he is just one of the herd.

The pain persists into the second day. He needs the pills. He longs for the voice, he longs for the arms. He doesn't know what would happen if he ran into them, but maybe the pain would stop. He knows he is thinking these things because he is irrational. He is weak. Not like them. And perhaps they are just trying to make him stronger.

In the afternoon, he reads the message on the pad again; he still doesn't understand. He places the pad on his chest and dozes fitfully on waves of pain.

He wakes up to the sound of cherry blossoms hitting the window. For a moment, he thinks the coterie is leaning over him, and he is terrified.

He remembers that he is in his bedroom and there are no blossoms. The pad has slid off his chest. He picks it up.

Be. Be free. Whee! Can't be. Now – Ow! Pain. See?

He stares at the screen. What is this? He doesn't know, but he does know that he should erase it.

In the early evening, when the pain becomes unbearable, he limps over to Jen's.

She has to help him up the outside stairs. "Pretend," she whispers. "In case they're recording."

But even with her strong arm around his waist, he can't stop grimacing.

Once they are safely in her room, she gives him a pill and pats his back until it takes effect. "They'll get bored," she whispers. "You just have to get it right."

But he does not understand how, and he is too sore and too tired to ask.

◊

He hears their laughter, the slam of the front door downstairs, and he feels unhappy, and then guilty. They are only having fun. They are made that way. He erases the words on the pad and pretends to sleep.

And today, they forget about him. A part of him feels sad he'll never belong, but as he starts to drift, the voice calls to him; he runs towards it into a forest of cherry trees, their soft blossoms caressing his broken body.

◊

"Imagine it hurting," they say, and Pocock bends back the big toe on his left foot.

They know he can feel, so why does he have to imagine? He keeps his mouth tight, straight.

"Does it hurt now?" they ask, more anxiously. "Try to imagine the pain," they say, and "Pain is a liar," they say.

He concentrates hard on the forest and the line on the machine doesn't go up.

"Imagine harder," they say. "Imagine! Imagine! Pain is in the brain."

They look so desperate, it's hard to know what to do. Jen said that you have to get it just right. But do they want him to scream or not? He bites his cheek until the inside of his mouth is like a bloody rag.

"Look at his eyes," says Tarquin. "You can tell from the eyes."

And they finally smile. "At this rate, you'll be like us one day," they joke.

Pain is just pain, thinks Anton. It's not real. It's all in the head. Nevertheless, it is making me feel unwell. It is making me want to scream.

"Let me have a go," says Pocock.

"Always so impatient, Pocock," says Marj.

Anton braces himself, but he can't stop the yell.

"Superb," says Tarquin. "You're the most sensitive we've ever had."

But Pocock looks displeased.

"Sorry," Anton says.

Pocock ignores him. "Pain, on a scale of one to ten?" he asks.

"Eleven," says Anton.

"Clever little bugger," says Pocock, and he hands him the pill.

Anton glances at the line on the monitor. It is almost ten.

◊

He thinks he might tell Jen about the forest, but, settled on her bed, he can't say the words, although he can almost feel the blossoms touching his skin, smell their scent.

When the tears come into his eyes, Jen says, "Don't you see, bub? They are not brave like you. They just don't feel pain."

"I can't. I can't—"

She puts her arm around him and strokes his back.

Jen slips him two painkillers as he leaves. "Just pretend it's hurting," she whispers.

◊

Anton lies in his room, confused and guilty. He's too weak. He can't go on. But it's important to the coterie, and he wants to help them. He starts at every sound. It's hard to predict when they'll come for him. You can never tell what they'll do.

In the afternoon, he hears their footsteps on the stairs. He swallows both the pills. He is hurting all the time now; whatever happens, they won't be wasted.

"Anton," they call. "Come down! Tests today." They sound so cheerful, it almost makes him happy.

◊

He lies on the table and pretends to wince, only a little. Sometimes, they like it when he doesn't complain. He's worried about his eyes. Will they be able to tell from his eyes?

They start on his fingers and he decides to scream immediately, although he is actually half in the forest, running towards the voice.

Marj is angry. "I told you, Pocock! You have to take it slower. He's too tender now."

The look Pocock gives him – as if he hates him – makes him want to cry. Anton is terrified he will notice his eyes.

And then he is weeping.

But they are delighted.

"Have an extra pill today," says Pocock. "We don't need them."

And they burst into pleased laughter.

"Come on, let's leave the little baby to recover," says Marj, and they trail out, excited. "Crying! Actual tears!" they say. "Can you believe it?"

Their delight reminds him of when he first came to the house, when they loved him more.

I have made them happy, he thinks. But I? I?

◊

He asks Jen to meet him at the herd café. The coterie would never go there; there is nothing much for them to do.

He's not like them. He loves the simplicity of a cup of plain tea and a slice of cake. He nods to the members of his herd as he goes in and they nod back, but there are not many of them left and the atmosphere is subdued.

He sits down with Jen at a corner table.

He feels ashamed about the crying. But Jen has seen it before and she still likes him. And the coterie seems to like it too, so maybe it's OK? He takes a deep breath and shows her the latest writing on the pad. She reads it, frowning.

> *Be. Be free! Not free, small, not really here at all. Edge, ledge. Jump. See? Free!*

"Oh, bub, bub," is all Jen says, and she squeezes his arm tightly.

Relief floods him. "Is there a forest, Jen?" he asks.

Jen looks angry. "Bub," she says, "we used to have dogs."

"Dogs?" he asks.

"You know, bub, those furry creatures. Not wild, tame. Pets."

"Yes, pets," he says. "I've seen pictures."

"And cats," says Jen. "We used to say 'It's raining cats and dogs'. Of course, that part never happened. It was just an expression."

"What happened to all the dogs and cats?"

"Don't you see?" says Jen. "To them you are like a cat. Or a dog. They are just having fun."

"Did we love the dogs?" he asks.

Jen slips off her shoes and shows him her crooked toes. "They'll forget to make you better," she says. And she starts to cry.

◊

If I jumped, I'd break my ankles, he muses as he thinks about the strange message on the pad. This almost makes him laugh. Jen managed to get hold of stronger pills and the coterie seems distant, as if they are standing behind glass. He forgets to pretend.

Tarquin bends over him and stares into his eyes. "He's not responding. He can't feel it."

Anton can see the panic in their faces.

"Of course he can, you idiot," says Pocock. "All of them feel pain," and he brings his hand down hard in a karate chop on Anton's stomach.

Before Anton can stop it, his hand, with its broken fingers, hits out at Pocock, hard, right across his stupid laughing mouth.

Despite the painkillers, Anton screams.

"Ha ha," laughs Pocock. "Now we are finally getting somewhere."

They are satisfied and leave him.

He has only hurt himself. He doesn't cry, he sobs. He sobs about his lost father and the forest he will never see, though it's probably all in his head. He sobs because he loves the coterie, though they do not love him. And because he cannot bear to hurt them, although they hurt him. It isn't their fault, really. They just don't understand pain.

He sobs most of all because he would like to nail each fucking little Jesus Christ god one of them to a cross. He would like to make them scream.

◊

Jen and Anton sit on her bed. He has typed the latest message from the imaginary father onto his pad. They read it together.

In the dark forest, there is fear, the blossoms barely breathing, but they do, they still do. I am, I am, they sigh in the trees, in the branches.

Jen switches off the pad and lies down. "Why don't you rest for a little while?" she says, patting the space next to her.

"Do you mind?" Anton asks, and he settles into the circle of her arms, held firm, his broken fingers splayed against her chest. The new pills she gave him are working splendidly and he feels no pain.

"If I can just make them happy, maybe they will let me go," he murmurs. But he forgets that he wants to go; he is lost in this dear moment of cherry blossoms and warm arms.

He pretends that his father is watching over him, he pretends that Pocock and the coterie love him, that he belongs to them and they to him. He imagines that Jen is his mother as she rubs his back.

"I'm so sorry, bub," she tells him, once he's fast asleep. She strokes his hair as the gaps between his breaths increase. "But you won't be afraid anymore, bub, you won't feel a thing."

When Death Is Over

I N THE TOWER, the flats have windows facing outwards, and windows facing inwards too, to let in more light. But the hollow core is filled with darkness: debris, and some say bodies – bodies that were thrown, bodies that jumped from the fifty-fifth floor, bodies that block out the light. The darkness crept up slowly until it reached as high as the fifth floor.

And those who live on the bottom floors have inner windows covered with junk. Ads stamped on packaging stare in at them, the same slogans every day, like a sordid and never-ending wish for something very far away. And their outer windows are sealed off too, against scavengers and thieves, so they live in a permanent night.

And they, perhaps not surprisingly, are the ones who sing outside on the empty lot, whenever they can spare the time, in their white cloaks, grasping their shepherds' crooks. They sing away the demons, they sing in the hope. They drink and take drugs and they sing.

◊

The rumour started from the bottom and gradually made its way to the top. The shepherds claimed they'd seen a falling man, a trail of stars behind him, through their dark windows.

Not that anyone usually believes them. But they told this story for free.

They said that his leg was bent, then straightened, then bent – some thought he had been a ballet dancer – as if he couldn't decide, or wasn't comfortable.

He must have been falling a hell of a long time to do that, I thought.

He never landed, they said.

I sit near the window, trying to catch the breeze, looking out over the city. It is sweltering, the sun high, the dark night unimaginable. The shepherds' singing rises up from the lot, reaching me on the forty-third floor, and it is like the relentless buzzing of bees, the same song over and over until I feel as if I will faint.

After death is over, I will . . .
After death is over . . .

It's Sunday, but weekends don't matter much here, except to the shepherds. You lie on the bed in the corner, my absent darling, lost to sorrow. But I've given up asking how you feel. Your pain seems to drift in the hot gusts of air and I can see, just by looking at you, that you might be preparing to leave this world again.

I stick my head out the window and stare down at the druggie choir singing together on their patch of grass, far below. The shepherds sway and sing around a giant cross quivering in the ground, oblivious to the pain of this earthly life, for a short while anyway.

"What are you lovely people doing in a place like this?" I shout. I know they can't hear me and I start to laugh, at myself, at them, at the absurdity of their prayers, like I'm a bird flying over who doesn't ever have to sort anything out. Nothing to do with me.

I don't laugh at you, of course, but then you have become like a stone on the bed and I know that you'll be like that for some time – forever, according to you. But you've cheered up before, and I can't take it too seriously, no matter how much I tell myself I should, I should.

We could go outside, join the choir. What difference would it make if we don't believe in the words? In your depressed state, you might believe in anything, even your own salvation. I make up a new song for them to sing to you. I shout it out the window, though neither they nor you are listening.

Go into the light
Crawl your way towards it
Go into the light

You stir and I shut the window, making our room into an oven. I imagine us moving to the first floor, where it would be impossible for you to open a window, let alone jump out of it. But I couldn't face the darkness. Or the druggies, once their compensatory piety has ended.

I lock the window, though it seems unlikely you will actually get up. Apparently, jumpers do it when they are halfway happy. Like you did. Tried to.

It could be worse, we could live on the top floor.

I lock the door, then take the lift down, enjoy the sinking in my stomach, the speed, the feeling of going somewhere – far away from here would be ideal.

There's a small crowd drinking outside the store on the edge of the lot, watching the shepherds on their knees. Nothing much else to do.

"Yea, though you walk," someone cracks.

But nobody ever touches them, not while they are in their cloaks at least.

I buy a few cans and join the crowd. I down one quickly, looking up to see if I can pick out our window, but it's a long way up and the sun is reflecting off the glass, piercing my eyes.

Rapunzel, Rapunzel . . .

But your hair is short now. You can't be bothered to wash it, and I'm too tired. I think of how lively you used to be.

I bump into Jomo in the lift. We stand smiling down at our feet. I know he fancies me. And I fancy him back. Just a little. A moment of guilt. But these moments are fading . . . I am losing you . . . slowly . . . You are losing me . . .

"How's your cousin?" he asks.

"Fine, fine, you know." More guilt. But you can't always tell the truth around here. How would he react if I told him that we're not cousins, but girlfriends?

"Just heard," he says, waiting for me to show some interest.

And I do. "What?"

"The falling man. The shepherds say it's like stars. We're stars falling behind him. Weird, huh?"

"Yeah, right," I say, and we both laugh. By now, everyone is talking about the falling man. He has been sighted enough times to become the most recent legend. There have been a few.

You are in the exact same place when I get back. I sit and stare out the window some more, sipping slowly to make the cans last. The choir has dispersed and there is just an empty field covered in rubbish and struggling grass.

How did we end up here?

I remember when you were a bright sunbeam, long hair and a cherry-red dress, garish lipstick. None of the heteros would have believed you were the one who was only into girls, girls, girls.

I think of Jomo. Never an option for you. It would be so easy to . . .

Not that easy.

I go into the kitchen to get another beer. A shaft of sunlight reaches towards the bottom of the inner core, but it's still dark down there.

We can't move down. We can't. We should leave before your savings run out. Go somewhere else. How? We can barely afford the forty-third floor on my wages. My family's too poor to ask, and yours, rich, but I think they're the reason you're lying here like a stone. Even if you refuse to admit it.

"They're too old to understand," I said.

I wish you'd never told them we're a couple. I could have lived without them knowing. I was happy to pretend to be your friend, cousin, whatever, forever. Now I'm all the family you've got.

You need to get better. You used to earn a lot more than me.

Pray, yea, OK, I can't think in this heat. I go back to the view and sing softly to you until the city lights twinkle on and the sky turns purple, the thunder drowning out my voice.

Go into the light, crawl your way towards it
Go into the light
I don't want to move to the bottom, no, no, I don't
Please get your fucking ass into the light!

It's not safe on the bottom floors at night, and the rain is pouring down, but I can't sit here doing nothing for much longer. What if I end up like you?

The lift is slow and almost stops a couple of times. I say a little prayer to a god I don't believe in and it keeps going. I make it to the shop and buy a few more cans, but it's late and the drinking has progressed. I ignore the leers and the pleas of the shepherds and their assorted hangers-on to stay, have a drink.

Just as the lift doors are closing, someone presses the button and they judder open. I breathe out in relief. It's only Louie, a preacher in the choir. An alky, but OK. He lives on the ground floor.

"Where you going?" I ask, checking he's not following in your footsteps. But he doesn't look like an aspiring jumper. Up to no good, more like.

His eyes are unusually clear – I wonder how long that will last – and they shine when he answers. "To the roof," he says. "To see him again. The falling man."

I just nod and wring out the bottom of my T-shirt.

"I need to see him. I wanna give up the juice, permanent, move up near the top."

I don't blame him. You'd never survive sober, living at the bottom.

"All the way to the top," I say, and I hold up my can and we laugh.

Nonsense of course, but I have to ask. "What did he look like?"

"Sad," he says. "Full of the world's sorrow."

I try to look encouraging. "And?"

"He was upside down, then the right way. Followed by stars. Us. Falling. He waves to nobody. He is shadows, man."

I force a smile. "Hope you catch him."

You have stretched out on the bed and look like you are actually sleeping. I drink my beers and watch the lightning cracking the sky apart. I can't stop thinking about him, this falling man, even though he doesn't exist.

He never reaches the bottom. Not like you.

Eventually, I lie down beside you, not touching. I close my eyes and listen to the wind whistling down the core, singing me to sleep.

Why have you left me here?
I'm alone in dark shadow, I am a shadow
The wind whispers over my head now
and I fall and I fall and I fall

It's Monday. Work day. So I pop next door to Angelo's to ask him to keep an eye on you. Rumour has it he's an ex-freedom fighter, soldier, something like that, retired on a small pension. He's all we've got. He's cheerful enough when I hand him a ten. As if we can afford it.

Please go into the light.

"Just unlock the window at eleven and three," I say. "And make sure you're there all the time it's open."

"Watch out for the falling man," he says.

"Ha ha, thanks, see you later."

It's a relief to be at my job a good few kilometres away – even if it is just a coffee shop – though I worry about you, but I do that when I'm at home, so . . .

I sing away, making coffee, making tea, grinning mock-grateful at some asshole who leaves me a ridiculously small tip. Between customers, I imagine the falling man. I can't go where I like, but I can imagine what I like. I can sing what I like.

It's pouring down all the way home. I can't wait to take off my wet clothes. Small pleasures.

There's a commotion on the lot, unusual for a Monday. A big crowd is standing in the rain, watching Louie waving his crook above his head. He looks demented; I can't tell if it's the drink or not. The choir is soaked but in full swing.

After death is over
I will fall, I will fall
I will be a shining star in your mantle of gold

He must have seen the falling man again. Why does everything have to be turned into religion?

Still, it's good to do something different, a free outdoor recital, wet, but at least warm. The rain washes over me and I close my eyes, swaying to the music, delaying the moment I have to get in the lift.

> After death is over
> Let me sing, let me sing
> Take away my loneliness
> Take away my sin

> Wrap me in your shadow
> So I do not feel again
> Take away my darkness
> Take away my pain

> After death is over
> I will fall, I will fall

I look up and count down from the fifty-fifth floor until I reach the forty-third. Then I count along, starting from the lift shaft, and you are leaning out of our window. I stare at your tiny face, imagining you lifting yourself up onto the sill.

I bolt to the lift, jab at the buttons. I run my hands through my wet hair, ignoring the two in the corner making a deal. They get out on the third floor. I jab some more. What was I thinking? Bloody falling man. Bloody Angelo. Bloody selfish you! How can you even contemplate jumping? Selfish, selfish, you might kill someone.

But when I get there, you are just looking out the window.

"It's raining," you say. "They are singing about him. I want to see him."

It's the first thing you've said for weeks. Hallelujah. Praise to the falling man.

But I'm not sure if this is a good sign; sometimes it's easier when you are a stone. I sit down on the couch and roll my eyes behind your back, arms crossed. I look over at the open window and swallow my fear. "Just popping next door," I say.

I knock on Angelo's door and gesture silently that I want to come in. He closes the door after us.

"The window was unlocked," I say.

He holds up the key. "It was locked when I left her."

"Shit!" I remember I left our spare key on the sill. "Sorry, sorry," I mumble, and I look at the ground. He pats me on the shoulder. I try to smile, but for once I can't.

"Don't worry," he says.

I nod, and go back to you. It's a relief to see you lying down again, rain coming in at the window. I sit with you and hold your hand.

You squeeze mine. "I heard the singing," you say.

After you are asleep, I lock the window and move to the kitchen so that I can stare through the inner window instead. I haven't opened if for a long time and the catch is jammed. I shove at it, and it gives suddenly, flinging open. I stick my head out; a couple of lights near the top outline the curve of the tower, but it's pitch-black at the bottom. At least I can't see the rubbish.

It's ridiculous, but yes, I'm waiting to see if there is actually a man. He only falls in the core, they say. I listen to the rain hitting metal, hitting plastic, hitting who knows what. Are there really bodies down there? We've all heard of a few jumpers. And a few who didn't exactly volunteer.

Next day, I lie in bed and think of calling in sick. I'm so tired, I do actually feel ill. But we need the money. I'm going to have to ask you about the key, I'm going to have to mention 'it'.

But you get up before me. I'm about to speak when you say, "It's too hot with the windows closed. I promise I won't jump," and you go into the shower.

I knock on Angelo's door.

"Don't worry about the cash today," he says. "I've got nothing else to do anyway."

I don't sing at work. I just watch the clock tick away, slow as can be, while I gulp down coffees.

When I get home, you are still in one piece. Angelo's there, and Petra from down the corridor. They are talking about, guess who. You look bleak, but you are listening. I'm not sure if it's doing you any good.

"I think he must be Nadeep," says Petra. "That one from the fourth floor who – When was it?"

I frown, but she carries on.

"Oh yeah, last Christmas. His wife ran away with his best friend. He stopped working, moved down a few floors. Started stealing, everything. You can't live down there and stay clean when you've got nothing to do."

"I heard he was a nice man," says Angelo.

"Yeah," says Petra. "It's never the ones you'd expect—"

She notices my expression. "Anyway, must be going."

"I don't think it's him," you say.

Everyone looks at you.

"How do you know?" asks Angelo.

"No one has seen his face," you say. "Could be anyone."

"Let's get some beer," says Angelo. "On me. Fucking army good for something, eh?"

I look at you and you nod. "Yes, stay. Cheers," I say.

I give up on the censorship. It probably won't make much difference to your mood anyway. We sit and drink cans and swap stories about the falling man, as if we're kids. It gets so late, or we get so drunk, we forget he's not real.

He's Jesus, he's the devil, he's Nadeep, no, he's Charlie, or maybe Thuli, or that bloke's mother who suffered from paranoia, or that guy who spent seven years putting his brother through school and the brother got stabbed the day before his graduation, or the CEO who lost his job and ended up moving here . . .

I must have passed out. When I wake up, you have taken my place at the inner window, but you are fast asleep and snoring, your head resting on your folded arms, the morning sunlight sinking down into the core behind you.

I get you up and into the bed and leave a glass of water next to it before I tiptoe out. My head hurts too much to worry today. Angelo is probably asleep too, and I doubt you'll wake up till this afternoon. You look utterly wiped, but in a good way, a normal way.

Jomo pops in for a coffee. "You look like shit."

"Thanks," I say, yawning, and give him, and myself, an extra shot.

"Want to maybe do something Friday?" he asks.

"Can't. Looking after my cousin."

He mock sighs and smiles. He looks gorgeous with his gleaming curls.

Should I just tell him about you?

"And anyway, don't you know there's a show on?" I say.

He's puzzled for a moment. Then he remembers the choir warms up for Sunday mass outside our building every Friday. "The shepherd show!" he says.

"You got it. Eight o'clock sharp."

When I get home, there's a bigger crowd on the lot, people just sitting around talking. No sign of the shepherds. I walk past, and feel myself sinking as I go up in the lift. You are on the bed, fast asleep. Just tired, I think, I hope. I lie down next to you and listen to the wind whistling in the core. It's seconds before the blackness closes over me.

I go down in the lift, singing; it feels good to be alive today. Maybe I really should join the choir. Your face is still so serious, but you woke up before me. You got dressed. You even brought me tea. I know, I know, it's happened before. But Angelo said you could go over to his place, listen to some records, and you actually said yes. Going anywhere is a good step. I'm starting to think of Angelo as the father I never had. And tomorrow's Friday. Maybe we can even go out, just for a little while.

Angelo rings at four, shortly before I knock off. "Looking bad," he says, "but I'm here until you get home."

I spend some more of our precious money on a cab. People call out to me as I rush past the lot. I wave and keep going.

Angelo sits next to the bed. You have changed from a stone to a river, tears flowing strong. Stupid me. What did I expect?

"Thanks," I say, and he gives me a hug and leaves us. Come back, I want to say.

I try to touch you, but you flinch away. I lock the inner window, then sit and listen to the choir, the sun sinking huge and orange behind them, your shape on the bed blurring into the dusk.

I will fall, I will fall . . .

If I could just save you, catch you, catch you on fire with life . . . If I could just make you happy . . . I'm caught, I'm falling . . . If I could just . . . save you, save me.

Next morning, you wake up and carry on crying. I call in sick.

The day goes by, a dull dream. You eventually fall asleep, and I feel trapped in this room like you are trapped in your head. By dusk, I'm practically ready to join the jumpers myself. Not really. Despite everything, I am cheered up by the tiny people, the human spirits whirling below in their white capes and hats. I can't help it. Thank God for distractions.

More and more people are exiting the tower to join the crowd outside. They drink and chat and watch the shepherds' white robes swirling under the street lights. Everybody knows of someone who fell. They are hoping to see the falling man, to be a part of him. To make it all better.

Am I like everybody else? You almost fell. I felt the dark wings of night rushing by, but I grabbed you by the back of your belt, just in time. My hands are so tired; it feels like I've been hanging onto you forever. But I can't let go now.

You are still here, and you wake up and you say, "They are singing," swiping your hand hard across your eyes.

I can see you are trying, for me. I go over and you let me hug you.

"I want to go down," you say. "I want to sing."

I don't ask if you're sure. "Hold my hand," I say, and we go down in the lift. Better than the window, huh, I think.

We get there as the disc of sun is disappearing, setting

the shepherds' cloaks on fire as they stand in a line, staffs raised, looking up.

He's in the core, if he's anywhere, you idiots, I think.

But you are clutching my hand so hard, I try to believe. In you at least.

There's excitement in the air; everyone is talking about the falling man. And I must be going mad myself because I dare him to appear. I imagine him falling: I am standing underneath, waiting to catch him. I want to gather him up, unbend his leg and hug him to me, to talk, soothe, anything.

He does not exist.

But you are going over to the shepherds and they shake their staffs and they cover you in a mantle of gold. A white cloak, actually, but it looks gold in the last gleam of the sun.

Jomo pops up beside me. Bad timing.

"My cousin," I say, pointing at you swaying and singing.

"At least there's dancing," Jomo says.

The wind is whipping the shepherds' cloaks, a big storm on its way. The lightning razors the skyline behind them as the city lights wink on and night descends. It feels like the tower looming above us has emptied its floors: the lot is packed with residents, drinking and mingling, some in suits, others in rags.

After death is over
I will fall, I will fall

People glance up from time to time, as if they really expect to see the man. The way they are knocking back all manner of stuff, some of them probably will. I keep my eyes on you, listening to snatches of conversation.

"I had a brother . . . Right from the top floor . . . Bastards threw him off . . . Nobody saw her, but we know she's in there . . ."

You look like a Jesus nut, your arms stretched out, your white robe flapping behind you. But you are up and you are singing and that is enough for me for now.

When death is over, over
How I fall, how I fall

The singing gets louder; it seems to wrap itself around the building, the wind howling along with it. If there is a falling man, they've probably frightened the life out of him.

Louie says a prayer and the crowd quietens down. But by the time the singing starts again, the lot is one giant party. People are playing music, laughing at the shepherds, getting bored and throwing cans.

"The falling man's a demon!" someone shouts.

I'm starting to feel crushed. I manage to find Jomo and Petra and Angelo near the entrance to the tower. "Let's go upstairs. I'll just get my cousin," I shout.

I don't want to be alone with you tonight.

I struggle through the crowd towards you. Some of the shepherds are starting to disrobe, but you are still singing away. "We have to go," I shout into your ear.

You shake your head, but then you open your eyes and look around, bewildered.

"Invite them up," I shout.

I gather you and Louie and a couple of the shepherds. The crowd is still good-humoured, but they want something to happen. "The man, the man," they cheer, as we push our way to the entrance. "Where's the falling man?"

It's quiet inside for a Friday night; we listen to the wind screeching down the core while we wait for the lift.

The others fetch their booze and we meet back in our flat.

"Let us pray," says Louie, and I go along with it because you look, not exactly happy, but better, much better.

The prayers don't last long, and then the staffs and cloaks are shed, the music starts, spliffs are rolled. Shouts drift up from the crowd below.

You are drinking, dancing with Jomo. You look OK, but I can't relax. I go into the kitchen and open the inner window. I pull up a chair and stick my head out into the dark core. I can feel the wind and rain on my face. I breathe in. I don't know if I can do this anymore.

"I want to see him," you say behind me.

I can't just give up on you. I gesture to the window, and you stand next to my chair as we lean out into the darkness, my hand hovering near your belt. I can feel your breath, warm on the back of my neck.

"Maybe one day I'll see him, hey?" you say, after what feels like forever.

I'm relieved, then worried, when you leave me. I watch as you recede into the warm light of the living room.

I turn back to the window and rest my elbows on the sill, my head in my hands.

Just darkness out there.

The longer I sit, the more bleak I become. The moon high above the core turns into a dark crust as the clouds pass over it, and I feel something coming, something that has been inside me for a long time. It creeps out, a dark shadow clutching my throat and whispering to me: you are not enough, you are nothing, you are alone.

I bow my head and give up. I can't keep hold of you the whole time.

I lean further out.

I feel him before I see him. The wind compresses above me. I look up and he is soft shadow falling.

Down and down he comes. Stars fall down after him. He is pain and shadow, falling, falling . . .

I reach out my arms to catch him.

And I feel the darkness. It sweeps through me like something crashing into being. Him in each of us, and us in him. But we will die sometime and he will fall forever.

I reach out and he slips through my fingers . . .

. . . falling, falling, a trail of us behind him, all the might have beens, twinkling, fading stars.

He sinks into the core and into that part of me I couldn't face in you.

Then he is gone, leaving only the soft yellow of stars to light the way.

I go back into the living room. You look at me and you know I've seen him. But it's like I'm sucking all the blackness from you, because your face illuminates into joy as I grow heavy as a stone. You touch my face. You wipe away my tears as the shepherds start to sing.

When death is over, over
How I fall, how I fall

I will never reach the bottom
I will feel no pain at all

I pour a big drink and stand looking out at the city lights,
the sirens below calling the falling man home.

Hooked

I T WAS FIRST spotted up in the sky, hanging from the hard steel hook of a crane. A woman in a fourth floor flat zoomed in her camera from two blocks away to take a photo.

Afterwards, she couldn't say why she did. It looked like all the other bits of metal dangling from the towering cranes crammed into the few miles around Old Street Station. The cranes were there all the time now, and why not assume it was just another steel girder waiting to be fitted into one of the half-built rooms that gaped onto the street?

Instinctively, she held the camera steady and pressed the button.

The photo came out dark, and it was only when she downloaded it onto her computer and applied a contrast filter that she saw what looked like a fish, its colour a deep blue with white speckles rather than metallic grey. A large eye was barely discernible.

The woman turned from the computer to look out again. Red lights flashed from the top of the crane, warning aircraft flying into London City Airport. Then she began to search the Internet, thinking it might be an art installation of some sort.

Nothing turned up, and the next day, waking early and it being Sunday, she set off to find the fish. She looped past housing estates and trendy bars and high-rises, the citizens of London still huddled in their beds, suspended and dreaming behind curtains and blinds. The woman shivered in the early spring air as loose associations ran through her mind: fish and chips, Pisces, pescatarians, glints of scales in deep water. The clouds moved fast, high above her head, slipping between the luxury blocks that had shot up like greedy weeds.

She was about to give up her search, when she entered a narrow Victorian alleyway and arriving at a small square, found a white van and a group of people in protective suits and gloves. It was not yet seven-thirty and nobody else was about.

Swinging from the hook in its mouth, above a large reinforced-styrofoam box resting on the cobblestones, was a fish the length of a person. Its deep blue colour had already faded to a dull brown. Four fleshy, limb-like fins stuck out from its body.

The woman leant against a wall near the entrance to the square. It can't possibly be real, she thought, it must be made of something like fibreglass, and she imagined it shattering into thousands of pieces. But she kept abreast of local events: if it was an installation, then why the lack of publicity?

Six white-suits surrounded the fish. They were struggling to manoeuvre it from the vertical to the horizontal as it was winched slowly down. They staggered and almost dropped it with anxious exclamations. It was obviously heavy.

The fish gave no sign of being alive. One cloudy, perfectly round eye stared at the woman, unseeing. She watched as the white-suits staggered again and nearly smashed its stout jaw against a corner of the box. But they kept hold of it and guided it to rest on its bed of ice. The fish seemed to be gripping the hook between its sharp, uneven teeth; they had to force open its small mouth to carefully remove it. They covered it with a plastic sheet, snapped the lid shut, and then stepped back to catch their breaths and stretch. One of them waved at the crane operator, and the hook rose slowly back into the sky. Making a last effort, they lifted up the box and carefully slid it into the back of the van.

The fish couldn't be made of fibreglass if it was so heavy, thought the woman. Unless that was part of the act? But there was no audience. Was it a rehearsal?

The sun slipped behind the clouds and the square sank into shadow.

The white-suits slammed the van doors shut. One of them drove the van slowly through the alleyway, almost scraping the paintwork, the rest following reverently, as if they were part of a funeral procession.

"Is it art, mate?" the woman asked the last of them as he passed.

The man just smiled.

◊

"Fishy business," said the papers the next day. To all appearances, the fish was a coelacanth. It measured just over two metres long and weighed a hundred and eighty pounds. Once believed extinct with the dinosaurs, living specimens had been found off the coasts of South Africa and Indonesia. The coelacanth's lobed fins made it a possible link in the evolution of fish to four-legged land animals. Where had the fish come from? And what was it doing hanging from a hook in the sky? DNA tests would start immediately.

◊

The woman usually went to bed at a sensible time, but that night she stayed up to gaze from her window at the empty hook, speculating on the origins of the fish. She guessed it was a publicity stunt by a corporation, probably to advertise seafood. But why choose an endangered fish that came from another time? Besides, coelacanths could not be eaten: they exude large amounts of oil and have a foul flavour, said the papers. As she eventually drifted into sleep in the dawn light, she felt a chasmic emptiness in her that she had no idea had existed.

For three mornings, the woman dressed for work, then walked to the square before the sun rose, without knowing why, her movements sleepy and exaggerated in the velvet thickness of the pre-dawn air. She entered the neck of the square like an ancient fish slipping into a dark, undersea cavern and gazed up at the hook. The crane's warning lights flashed on and off far above her, like mysterious ocean creatures seen from the depths.

She slept less and less, and when the dawn came, she leant against a wall and shut her eyes to doze as the early-morning sunlight reached down to warm her face.

She stayed until the crowds began to trickle in, a mixture of workers, students, the unemployed, and the ubiquitous London tourists. They pointed their cameras at the hook swinging high above them, a cacophony of pings filling the square as they uploaded their images to social media.

The woman walked straight to the office from the square. She checked the papers as soon as she arrived. The only news of the fish was a brief article saying the DNA results had been delayed.

On the Friday morning, she leant against the wall of the square, eyes closed in a waking dream. She forced open her heavy lids, but could not make the effort to look up. As she gazed, half-seeing, at the cobblestones, something shiny caught her eye, something almost not there. Below the spot where the fish had hung was a dusting of translucent rainbow colours. After checking that no one was coming, she walked over and bent down to look closer. The patch of colour glinted and danced, as if beckoning her, before fading away in the brightening light. She heard the ring of high heels on cobblestones and hastily left the square.

The woman waited impatiently for the coming night. In the early hours, once the streets had cleared, she entered the square, her hand half-covering her torch to dim the beam of light. She knelt down and, yes! She had not imagined it. The rainbow colours still burnished the cobblestones, like scattered sunlight penetrating deep water.

Unsure of what to do next, she stood under the empty hook, feeling again the unfamiliar and vast emptiness. Her eyes began to close. And just then her torch caught another patch of colour, and then another. She shook herself awake and followed the patches back along the alleyway.

They were scarcely visible and she had to stop often to find the next one. The sky was heavy with cloud, but as she went on, her eyes adjusted to the murky dark and the vibrant traces fused into a shimmering trail. Somehow, she knew she would find the fish at the trail's end. Dreamily, she followed it, feeling her heart lift as she glided along a busy road, through a park, past the ministry of something or other, where outcomes and evaluations seemed to drift out into the night air, then vaporise; and she laughed as she would have in a dream.

All night, she circled the hushed streets of London, following the rainbow trail, but it went on and on and she could not stay awake.

She woke in her bed late that Saturday afternoon, with no memory of how she had got there. Over coffee, she read the breaking news on her tablet.

"Coela-can-be!" proclaimed the papers. The DNA tests were complete. The fish was a genuine coelacanth. And it did not belong to the two extant species. The tests would be redone. Meanwhile, the hunt had started for the pranksters who had somehow found the fish and hauled it into the London sky.

Social media ignored the evidence and speculated the fish was a fake, the work of a copycat Banksy. But what did it represent? the Londoners asked each other. The fish hung in their minds, suggesting possibilities resting just out of reach.

The fish's location was not disclosed in the reports.

The woman was determined to resume her search that evening, but instead she fell into a deep and dreamless sleep as soon as darkness fell. She woke late on Sunday morning, annoyed with herself for wasting a whole night. After a day of restless fidgeting, she called in sick and took a week off work.

Something compelled her to start her search from the beginning. She returned to the square and lingered, half-looking at the ground, until she found the patch of colours. And then she began her long walk, tracing the shimmering path through the streets of London in ever-expanding circles that joined to form a spiral. But she searched for the fish in vain, waking in her bed, not knowing how she had got there.

It wasn't until the next night of walking that she managed to stay awake by pinching her arms and rubbing her eyes. She reached as far as the north bank of the River Thames. And there the trail ended.

A fresh breeze blew in off the waters. The woman stood, cold and alone in the dark. She would never find the fish, she thought. She squeezed her eyes shut to keep from crying. Thought left her and yet again she felt the strange emptiness, before faint dream fragments began to drift up into consciousness.

She opened her eyes and the trail was right in front of her. It continued up a wall to the first-floor window of a dilapidated, old, red-brick building. A small sign above the entranceway said: Marine Museum.

The fish is inside, thought the woman, but immediately her eyes grew heavy. And as she dreamt, standing upright, the trail thickened into a cascade of colours that gushed out of the window and down the wall. The woman swayed as the current swirled around her feet, pulling her this way and that, before it rushed back along the spiral and flooded the city.

It was as if the fish, displaced to the sky, had brought with it dense dreams from the depths. Waves of rich colour unspooled through its gills and seeped into buildings, drifted in through windows, crept under doors and up staircases and into people's bedrooms, where they lay sweetly sleeping or loudly snoring, reaching even hardened criminals in their cells. Lost children, huddled together in doorways, stirred and smiled. And all of them were filled with a wondrous sense of home.

All night, the rainbow tides surged through the brains and bodies of the Londoners, before the coming of the rosy dawn, and they woke with a feeling of mysterious ancestry. They smiled to themselves on their way to work, but did not talk of their strange new happiness. It was ungraspable, a sense of something missing, now filled in, and they could not put it into words. Besides, they were not used to talking to each other. It was just a silly dream, they told themselves as the day wore on and their new-found happiness ebbed slowly away. And they bent their heads once more to their desks.

The woman could not remember leaving the river when she woke in her bed at home. For two more nights, her feet led her along the spiral to the museum. For two more nights, the colours swirled around her, and the Londoners slept and dreamt and woke in warm bliss. Their days began in a dreamy satisfaction and they almost smiled at strangers on their way to work. They stared out of windows, watching new leaves unfurl on the trees, and longed for the night. But still they did not speak of their dreams to each other, and by the end of the workday, they had forgotten them.

By the Thursday night, the woman was exhausted. Her clothes hung on her thinning frame as she tramped the spiral alone. When she reached the museum, she caught an unpleasant whiff of oil from the window. But her longing to see the fish had become overwhelming. Before her body could betray her with sleep, she stepped under the window and deliberately immersed herself in the rushing tide of colour.

A feeling of completeness overtook her as she entered a dark, buoyant dream world, gliding and flicking through uncanny swells along the sinuous Thames, heading out to deep sea. She felt the tumult of blood under scales, the tides thrumming in her body like heartbeats, and the swish of water sliding through her gills. Then she flew through the air, the hook digging into her mouth behind her sharp, uneven teeth. A cold breeze swung her from a crane, the pressure of the air insubstantial on her hard scales. "Return me to the water," said a disembodied voice.

That night, the Londoners dreamt of being engulfed by giant waves. They cried out in their sleep as they sank into dark, unknowable depths.

The woman did not wake in her bed, but in the square. As she made her way home, an unease hung in the air. All along Old Street, dazed, tired Londoners staggered to work, gazing worriedly into the distance.

When they finally reached the office, they settled in at their computers and tried to forget their dreams, only to find themselves, by afternoon teatime, leaping up from their desks, or daring themselves to stay still, when their minds plunged into deep watery caverns and chthonic sea snakes rippled across their toes.

By the following day, a Saturday, a thick soup of dark dread and vivid imaginings merged with the London smog. People gathered outside, open-mouthed. They held out their hands, grasping at elusive signs and symbols, closing their fists on air, or ran for cover, desperate for concrete particularities. The line between day and night, the ordinary and the extraordinary, began to fade.

The mayor was at a loss. "It is not clear . . . Where does it stop and start?" she asked during a special broadcast, before flinching in fright as something rustled to her left.

That night, the woman's feet were bruised and sore. She stood outside the museum, wide awake, yet exhausted. The oily smell was now pungent and terrible, and she kept herself apart from the stream of colours.

But the smell was inescapable; it stung her nostrils with the fish's desperation to return to water. She held her nose and, for a second time, she forced herself to step under the window and into the stream.

"I have been hooked," said the dream voice.

At that, the stream of colours stopped, and the whole of London woke from a troubled sleep and sat up in their beds.

Seized with a sudden energy, the woman knew exactly what to do.

She frantically jiggled the rusty handle of the low museum door, but it was securely locked, and she ran along the towpath until she found a wooden barrel in a pub garden. She rolled it under the museum window and heaved it upright, before clambering onto it.

Through the locked window, she saw into a small room with white walls. The hump of the fish lay on a metal table, under a transparent plastic sheet. She jumped down and searched behind the building. She found a section of pipe in an old bucket and used it to thump against the thick glass, until it imploded and a rush of freezing air burst out into the night. Carefully, she knocked out sharp slivers of glass, before climbing through the window onto the hard floorboards.

The woman stopped for a moment to look at the ancient fish, lying cold on the table, and was filled with an unbearable sadness.

The door to the room opened onto a narrow, wooden staircase. She unlocked the door at the bottom, then fetched the bucket. She crossed the towpath and, clinging onto a railing, she made her way down a set of stone steps, slippery with moss, leading to a tiny beach on the Thames. The wide, swelling river roiled and shimmered, the incoming tide lapping over her feet as she filled the bucket. Bent double with the weight of the water, she staggered back up to the room where the fish lay.

Gently, she pulled the sheet from the coelacanth's body. She longed to touch it, but knew she shouldn't. Instead, she poured the water slowly over its dull brown scales, starting from its tail.

As she poured, the fish began to turn a deep, glistening blue. By the time she reached its head, her arms trembled with effort, and she accidentally slopped some of the water into its mouth. The sound of the sea swishing through its gills reached the woman as if carried to her by a deep, underground current. She poured in the last of the water, and the fish unhinged its jaw and opened its mouth as wide as it could go. The dream trail of sea snakes and waves and happiness began to slide back into it, and its blue colour became so dazzling that the woman could not look at it directly.

The fish rose from the table and swam out the window by instinct, something stirring in its fatty brain.

It made no sense and it made some sense.

And as it flew over London, the Londoners rose from their beds and went out onto the streets. They stood together, rich and poor and in-between, looking up in stunned silence as the fish swam in circles above them, gathering the rainbow trail up into its body.

The fish completed its spiral near London Bridge. And then, as suddenly as it had arrived, it dived deep into the Thames, stray dreams escaping from its gills and separating into strands of colour in a sunrise over the water, the like of which had never been seen in the great city of London. All along the banks of the river, to the very mouth of the Thames, the rainbow colours saturated the sand on the small beaches exposed by the withdrawing tide, and the waters were lit as if by New Year's Eve fireworks.

Gradually, the sky took on its usual colour as clouds covered the sun, and a great sadness descended.

Overcome with grief, the woman hardly knew what to do. Wide awake, she made her way back to the square along the now invisible spiral, each step seared with pain. She found that she knew the way by heart. When she entered the square, the crane and the hook were gone.

For the rest of the day, she sat slumped against a wall, staring up at the empty sky, until night began to fall and she could hardly stay awake.

As she left, already half-dreaming, she thought she glimpsed the dim outline of a fish on the wall to the left of the exit.

The next day was Monday. The woman checked her tablet as soon as she woke.

There was no news of a dazzling-blue flying fish, or of a fantastical sunset. But a tourist had discovered a fossilised coelacanth embedded in the wall of the square. Of course, said everyone on social media, it must be Banksy after all.

And for the rest of that day, awash in a strange melancholy, the Londoners talked to each other about the fish and shared their strange dreams. Doctors listened to their patients for hours, children were allowed to read all day at school, while teachers threw heaps of forms into the recycling. Shopkeepers absentmindedly handed out free packets of biscuits and crisps with stunned expressions. Traffic slowed, and then stopped, the sound of hooting noticeably absent as drivers left their cars to take turns on couriers' bicycles. The usual thick band of pollution hanging over London lifted up into the air and disappeared. Stockbrokers rubbed sticky tears from their cheeks, like sleepy children, openly weeping for forgiveness, and MPs leant out of windows, planning ambitious new parks, their minds expanded in ways they'd thought wholly impossible.

And as they went about their business, the Londoners felt the layers of clay and silt below their feet, as if they belonged to something even more ancient than this place they called London.

Banksy left a message, denying it outright. The council announced they would excavate the fish and exhibit it in a museum, but the public protests went on and on. Eventually, the authorities left it alone.

Sometimes, the woman walked the spiral to remind herself. And when the Londoners visited the square at night, they touched the fish reverently and remembered their visions as they stood in the dark. They smiled at each other. Then they went home to tell new stories.

Barleycorn

THE STUDENT SITS on her tiny balcony in the early autumn sunshine, high up above the endless, spreading city. She stares at the open laptop on the table in front of her. Her thesis, 'Climate Action: Theoretical Perspectives', stares dully back at her. Almost there, she tells herself. Again.

She scrapes her chair round and tips it forward to rest her head against the railings. Central Avenue stretches in a straight line from her building, City Park distorting it into the oval bulge of a satiated python about halfway down, where the road splits before rejoining and continuing on to the hospital.

Only the conclusion left to write and it'll be done. But she can't concentrate. Instead, she counts the dots of greenery below, florets of colour on dying concrete reefs, until her head slumps sideways, and she dozes and dreams of a wild and hairy man who bursts from a wood and chases after her, angry she is writing something he doesn't understand.

What a weird little man, she thinks when she wakes. Dreams are so funny. She shivers. Clouds move in, casting dampening shadows. The sky turns grey and flat as red tail lights streak the avenue below, nuzzling their way round the bump of the park, then onwards through the gloom.

She forces herself back to the laptop. Just over a week till her deadline. Uncharacteristically, her mind won't cooperate. She goes inside when it starts to drizzle.

◊

The drizzle continues into the night; it falls in soft veils, smudging the lights from the soaring tower blocks, it soaks into concrete, staining it dark brown.

In the early hours, the student gives up on the latest – not working – version of her conclusion, and goes to bed.

Not far away, in the basement of the hospital morgue, a forensic pathologist is taking tissue samples from a right arm. Fresh and neatly severed, complete with hand and fingers, it was found in an empty flowerpot in a rooftop garden. Tests have confirmed the victim's sex as male.

Short of sleep, as always, the pathologist resists the urge to scratch his stubble with his gloved hands. He runs a finger down the man's forearm – the skin is rough and deeply tanned. An outdoors type. Not even the room's cold temperature and the sharp chemical smell of disinfectant can hold off the cheesy-sweet whiff of incipient decay. He wrinkles his nose and takes off his gloves to type up his notes.

He downs an espresso from the machine in the corridor before driving home with his window open, enjoying the gentle rain slanting in onto his face. The earthy smell reminds him of the farm where he grew up. He can see the fat, golden heads of barley drooping towards the ground. They will be bringing in the harvest soon.

The pathologist hangs up his keys, wondering, as usual, why hooks are needed when there's a perfectly good table below them, then tiptoes through the house and into his back garden so as not to wake his husband. He gives his habitual half-smile at its ridiculously small size.

Rain drips onto his head as he shelters under a barren apple tree and smokes an illicit cigarette, daylight barely managing to push through the grey. He feels an odd stirring as he thinks about the dead man's tanned skin. Memories from childhood: running wild through the fields; later, driving the combine harvester, the rich gold stalks falling before being sucked into the machine, the chaff turning the sky dusty.

He recalls how, as he grew older, he'd been desperate to escape the visceral reality of stinking cow shit and fat flies. He smiles.

He is deciding whether to smoke another, when his phone rings. A second arm has been found by an office cleaner, in a flower bed outside an underground station. From the photo, he judges it's a likely match: cleanly severed, tanned, with a left instead of a right hand on the end of it. "Got to get some kip. I'll come in early after-noon," he tells the coroner.

He smokes the second cigarette, his tired mind grasping at something he can't quite see yet, a familiar feeling he doesn't try to push.

◊

The student wakes as the pathologist falls abruptly into a deep sleep. She dresses quickly, then runs down seven flights of stairs to buy the morning newspaper, as if escaping the hairy man from her dreams, who had chased her for a second night. Faster this time. And angrier.

She likes to buy a physical newspaper, a childhood ritual. The drizzle continues. She stays indoors and reads about the discovery of the first arm over a strong coffee. She feels safer knowing it belongs to a man. And then guilty about the poor dead man. But perhaps he's still alive, if one-armed?

She should start on her thesis. She drinks a second coffee and switches to her phone for more news. The man is definitely not alive. As people make their way to work under umbrellas, live updates of newly discovered body parts flood in from all over the city: two legs, with feet and toes, one found at the bottom of a fountain, the other lodged in a tree on a traffic island; a torso in a car park.

◊

By the time the pathologist wakes at noon, his phone is crammed with messages. He makes a quick coffee and forgets his freshly popped-up toast while he scrolls through them.

He puts his cup in the sink, wipes the spilled coffee, imagining his husband's pleased surprise. He has a hunch the parts belong to the same man, but he'll have to verify that.

He drives to work early, flicking on his wipers when the rain grows heavier. The harvest will be ruined if the rain carries on like this. The familiar pang of guilt at leaving the farm, his parents' disappointment.

Cocooned in the morgue, he examines the parts, separated from each other on cold metal tables to avoid cross-contamination. Every part of a man, including the internal organs, is there. Everything except the head. Unusual for them to be found above ground. In plain sight. Did the killer run out of time to bury them? Couldn't have. It would have taken time to dump them so far apart.

As he moves the bloody heart from the scales to the table, the weight of it resting in his cupped hands grows heavy and seems to pull him down into darkness. A memory, indistinct, a man in a field of barley, who was also not a man, who was the howling wind, who was chaff scratching at his eyes. An uneasy feeling follows: the parts, if laid out in the right shape, will somehow come back to life.

He focuses on labelling the samples for analysis. He'd thought his career had long since cured him of his youthful visions.

For once, he leaves work before it gets dark.

◊

The student rereads her concluding chapter for the tenth – eleventh? – time. The arguments are all there but somehow unconvincing, as if they add up to less than their parts.

She doesn't notice the gradually dimming light until she glances up and the sky is black. Any excuse for a break. She goes out onto the balcony. The rain falls more insistently as dense clouds bank up over the city and birds dive for cover. The wind hurtles between the towers, sending hollow knocking sounds echoing into the dark. Thunder rumbles closer. She sniffs the sweet, pungent smell of ozone, feels the tension, something gathering itself—

She ducks at the boom of thunder, a split second before a gigantic lightning bolt bursts open the sky as if it were a ripe fruit, illuminating the skyline with a blinding white flash, and no one sees the shower of gold seeds scattering to all corners of the city.

And then the rain hammers down with such force that cars pull over to the side of the avenue, their hazard lights blinking.

The student is soaked, but she laughs as she leans her full weight against the door to close it. She sits, wrapped in a towel, absorbed by the storm, her thesis forgotten.

◊

The rain falls hard all night. By the time the pathologist wakes, well after noon, the wind and rain have scoured away the usual grime and rubbish, as if clearing a path for something.

In the early evening, the pathologist gives himself up to the mellow autumn warmth as he drives to work through the steam rising from the tarmac. The sun is setting at a leisurely pace, suffusing the sky with an eerie, luminous gold.

As he gets out of the car, the windscreen wiper catches the sun and gleams. Buried memories tug at him, a man, no, something like a man, insects serenading the end of summer in a stubbled field . . . He bends closer. A gold barley seed is lodged in the wiper's rubber. He plucks it out and taps it against his teeth. Solid.

An image flashes into his mind: a severed head, its hair a tumbled, golden sheaf, its eyes a ferocious sky blue. He'd heard a scream above the harvester's engine as he mowed down the last swathe of barley. He'd looked over his shoulder and—

How can he have forgotten?

He pushes the seed into a corner of his wallet.

A ray of sun penetrates the darkened morgue through the narrow pavement window. He hesitates at the door, not wanting to turn on the searingly bright lights just yet.

The darkness reminds him of sitting in the farm kitchen. His father had eyed the empty rafter where the corn dolly usually hung, tied with a red ribbon, then plonked the mug of harvest ale down in front of him without a word.

Absurd tradition! The nature spirits are about as real as Father Christmas. So why does he still feel so guilty about not leaving them the last sheaf?

He goes over to the window and stands in the sunshine with his eyes closed. A wave of nostalgia for summer washes through him, tinged with deep sadness, as if it might never come again. And then the vision that haunted him for years: a severed head returning to its body, a man's parts miraculously joining back together.

He flicks on the lights. Once the work is finished, the unjoined man will be stored a while longer, then buried if nobody claims him.

◊

The student's vigour disappears along with the rain; she'd woken several times in the night when the hairy man chased after her, still infuriated about her thesis. He had a sickle now and was trying to cut off her head.

Dreams don't mean anything. But all day her thoughts return to the wild man as she edits and re-edits her conclusion. Her sentences feel wrong somehow, as if a layer of air separates them from reality.

◊

By the time the pathologist gets in, his husband has left for work. He goes into the back garden and taps a cigarette from the pack. The flooded soil and torn bushes shine wild and vivid with an hallucinogenic quality that corresponds to his trance-like state. Sleepily, he brings the cigarette to his mouth, enjoying the warm sun on his back. He cups his hand to light it and feels soft hair. *I must shave.* But as he moves his hand over his chin, an inner voice is already shouting, it can't be, it can't be, even as he feels the inches of silky hair.

He runs indoors to the bathroom mirror. The hair covers his entire face in tight whorls. He doesn't recognise himself as he tugs at it, already imagining googling a number for emergency electrolysis, wondering how he can get to an appointment without being seen.

He goes into the bedroom. Keeping his back to the full-length mirror, he strips off with his eyes closed, avoiding direct contact with his body, desperately hoping he won't find what he already senses he will. It takes him a few seconds to force himself to turn around.

The silky hair covers his entire body. He laughs in a short, hard burst, before tears seep through his furry cheeks to the skin underneath.

Outside, it begins to drizzle. He hides in the walk-in wardrobe, where he finally falls asleep.

◊

In the late afternoon, the student eventually gives up on her thesis. She decides a walk might help and sets off down the pavement that runs along the avenue.

◊

The pathologist wakes from a nightmare with a scream.

Wind howls over a barren field. Rain starts to fall, and he knows that summer will never return as a headless man rises from the ground and lifts his rough, tanned hands to where his missing head should be.

And then a few seconds of half-awake forgetfulness, until he feels the odd frisson of hair on hair where his arm rests against his cheek.

He realises he's still in the wardrobe. He lies stupefied. *How can I do my work like this?* It requires deft fingers for a start, and his are covered in matted hair. He shakes them furiously, unconsciously hoping to slough off the hair, but it makes no difference. A wave of shame suffuses his formerly smooth body. *I'm a freak! No one will take me seriously.*

But he is a practical person. He calls his husband. He

has to warn him. If he comes home to find a hairy man crouching in the living room, he might call the police. It goes through to voicemail. He hangs up. What can he say?

There is no fucking way he's calling in sick. Besides the excess hair, he feels fine. He refuses to miss out on helping to solve the case of the headless man.

◊

As the student walks down the avenue, checking the pavement for puddles, the metal skeletons of proliferating tower blocks, cramming in on both sides, don't give her much hope for the future. She can't quite acknowledge the feeling that there is no easy answer to the failure of humans to act on the environment. All that money, all that poverty, and the earth collapsing, while new strides are being made towards commercial travel to other planets. What is the point of studying? What is the point of theory?

◊

The pathologist phones in to say he'll be late for work. After dark, he shaves his face, pulls on a high-necked jumper, gloves, and a cap, then drives to the morgue. He strokes his face, compulsively checking for new growth. Instinctively, he avoids well-lit streets. He has a dreadful feeling that if anyone sees him, they'll mistake him for a dangerous animal and attack. *A small yeti?* Laughter bursts out of him for the second time since he became hairy.

He parks in front of the hospital, instead of in his usual spot in the underground garage. He leans back against the headrest. How to avoid the scrutiny of the security guards at the side entrance leading to the basement? His swipe card should still work. But if they so much as glimpse his face . . . He pictures them shooting him in the back as he runs down the corridor. He waits until several people enter the hospital before springing from the car.

He is looking down as he rushes across the pavement and doesn't notice the student walking straight towards him, deep in thought. They collide with such force that he forgets he's covered in hair. His cap falls, his scarf unravels. He sees disbelief and horror on her face as she holds her hands high in the air.

"Don't hurt me," she shouts, before she turns and bolts down the avenue.

◊

The student runs all the way home and up the stairs. If the hairy man had not been blocking the entrance to the hospital, she would have run right into it. In retrospect, she's glad she didn't. It appears her dream has come to life. How the fuck to explain that? She locks the door and pushes the kitchen table across it.

◊

The pathologist uses the shock of the collision for courage. Before he can think twice, he shoves his cap back on and winds his scarf tightly around his face. Head down, he makes it through security, grunting a greeting. At least his voice hasn't changed.

As he walks down the corridor, trying to appear casual, the feeling he could be shot in the back only gets worse. But he rushes down the basement stairs and pushes open the morgue door, unharmed. And there is the man, lying in parts in metal drawers. Of course he can never be put back together.

But his vision disagrees: he sees the man whole again, gold spreading from his heart in flaming fingers . . .

The head lying in the cropped field . . . Thank God he'd forgotten it . . . Was that why he left the farm?

For fuck's sake, pull yourself together! He places a Do Not Disturb notice on the door. He carefully shaves his fingers with a scalpel, then gets to work.

It is a few hours later, when he turns on the radio, that the news brings relief, as well as new horror. He is not alone. Dozens of people have been to their doctor's or A&E after sprouting a sudden and uncomfortable amount of hair. Scientists are speculating on a mutation caused by an unknown environmental factor.

But knowing he isn't alone doesn't help the shame. What if it turns out to be irreversible? He can't imagine living with a permanent pelt. Perhaps he could join the herd, or the troop, or whatever a group of excessively hairy people is called?

Despite his strong urge to give up and go home to bed, when he looks at the man lying in pieces in front of him, he knows he can't. *Who is he? What is he?*

He calls the coroner. "I'm one of the hairy people," he says. "But I'm fine. Of course, it won't affect my work."

The coroner is still laughing when he says, "I'm coming

down later to check up on you, hairy man. Shall I bring my clippers?"

◊

The student hardly sleeps. Each time she drifts into dreams, the hairy man runs from the wood, with his sickle, and jolts her awake. She makes coffee just after dawn, eyeing the table across the door as she sips it, her body tense, waiting until a decent hour to phone her mother.

"Have you read the news?" her mother asks.

"Not yet. Why?"

"You haven't heard about the hairy people?" Her mother explains that, so far, around fifty people have come forward.

The student is immensely relieved to hear a rational explanation for the hairy man she saw outside the hospital. She tells her mother about the collision and her dreams.

"The ancient wild man," her mother says. "He's trying to tell you something."

"What does it mean?"

"Dreams are personal. You have to work it out for yourself."

The student rolls her eyes and immediately regrets telling her mother. She doesn't share her belief in dream analysis and resents the knowing tone in her voice.

But after she hangs up, she can't help trying to interpret the dream. What if it means she'll become hairy. *Don't be silly.* But actual people have turned hairy, and the wild man in her dreams is chasing her, catching up. What will happen when he does?

She rereads the news, then checks every part of her

body for excess hair: nothing. In any case, she reasons, in the reports the hairiness started suddenly, the day after the storm.

She goes onto the balcony, uneasy. What if the hairiness is a punishment – *wrong word!* – no, an unstoppable consequence of environmental destruction? What if the entire human race becomes hairy? And how come she dreamt about the hairy man before she knew he existed?

She stares at the hospital at the end of the avenue. A sudden insight comes: the hairy man she'd run from was trying to get into it. Maybe he, or someone at the hospital, knows what's going on.

◊

Curled up on the couch, the pathologist pulls the duvet over his head and pretends to sleep. His husband is uncharacteristically late leaving for work. *Just bloody go! Please.*

But he comes over and sits near his head. "Anyone in there?"

The pathologist keeps his eyes closed.

His husband gently pulls back the duvet to expose the pathologist's face. The pathologist can imagine his expression from the incredulous tone of his voice when he says, "We need to get you to the doctor."

The pathologist notes that his husband leaves without trying to wake him. But he's right: he has to do something. He puts on kitchen gloves to avoid looking at his hands, then googles 'hairy people'. Somebody has already created a closed Facebook group called Excess Hair Support. *Hair Apocalypse, more like.*

Just press Join. But he can't bring himself to send the request. What if it's a hoax? And what the fuck sort of profile pic would he use? A before-and-after? He googles impatiently, ignoring the blinking ads for epilators and hair removal creams, until he comes across a government request asking people to register their hairiness with their GP or call a special hotline. He slams the laptop shut.

◊

The student wakes from yet another dream about the hairy man. Exhausted, she walks slowly downstairs to buy the paper. She peers cautiously down the avenue, half expecting to see the real-life hairy man running towards her from the direction of the hospital. By the time she's back upstairs, not even a fourth coffee can stop her from falling asleep.

The wild man rushes from the forest towards her, pointing his sickle at her head. Pain rips through her feet as she races over stubbled barley. A scream. She sees a man standing headless in City Park. He holds up his hands to where his head should be. "Dig!" says a voice.

She wakes frightened and disorientated and she knows – how? – that she must find the hairy man.

As the student strides through the ring of trees on the edges of the park, she smells wet grass and the sweet perfume of crushed lavender above the stench of car fumes. Although she feels continuously anxious about the future of the earth, she realises she hasn't really paid much attention to actual plants before. But now her despair feels connected to the muddy grass and scattered branches. "Soon, you too will be destroyed," she mutters.

◊

The pathologist has completed his tests on the man and is typing up his notes when the coroner comes in.

"Jesus motherfucking Christ!"

They stare at each other, awkward.

The pathologist breaks the silence. "Did you bring the clippers?"

At the reassuring sound of the pathologist's voice, the coroner gesticulates at him, suppressing a grin. "You look like a fucking caveman."

"They're less hairy."

They laugh.

The pathologist catches him up on the case: No match to known fingerprints or missing persons. No head.

"All set then," says the coroner.

It is soothing to maintain their old pattern; the pathologist feels almost normal. The coroner leaves to inform the security guards about him.

He waits for a while, then wraps up and goes outside for a smoke, ducking his head and mumbling hello as he passes their intensely inquisitive gazes.

◊

Don't think, don't think, the student keeps telling herself, and this gets her as far as the opposite side of the road to the hospital entrance, where she waits, unsure what to do next.

Half an hour later, she decides to go inside. *And ask what, exactly?* But, just as she is crossing the road, the hairy man comes out of the building; she recognises the green cap tilted forward over his face. He stares at the ground as he lights a cigarette.

"Hi. I, I knocked into you the other day. Sorry. I got a fright . . . I was wondering if . . . I had this dream . . ."

He doesn't look up.

"About a hairy man. He was chasing me. He was trying to cut off my head. Then a man was lifting up his hands. His head wasn't there—"

He looks up. Only his eyes show, tufts of hair around them.

Everything normal, thinks the student. *Except for the hair. Human eyes. Human!*

He sticks out a gloved hand.

She shakes it too hard, her fingers trembling. "I thought maybe – I don't know. None of this makes sense."

"Telling me," he says in an ordinary, human voice, pushing aside the bottom of the scarf to smoke.

She tells him about her dreams as he smokes a second cigarette, the lit tip dangerously close to the hair on his chin.

The student says goodbye. She looks over her shoulder and waves at the pathologist as she walks back down the avenue, his number in her phone.

"Call me if you have any new dreams," he'd said.

Even if a part of her remains sceptical, she knows that she will.

◊

The rain continues to fall and the student struggles to write. She goes out onto her balcony often. She feels a pressure building in the air, as if something wants to spring from City Park and flatten the encroaching concrete.

It is a few days later that the dream changes.

The student stands in City Park. She lifts up her hands, and her head is missing. A group of hairy people emerge from the trees and stand in a circle around her. "Dig!" says a voice. Frantically, she pushes a spade into the soft earth.

She wakes, frightened. She almost gives in and calls her mother to ask for an interpretation. She puts on more coffee instead. *It's just a dream.* But after her second coffee, she texts the pathologist.

◊

The pathologist places the man's parts in a cold storage unit. The parts are finally together. Minus the head. He resists the temptation to arrange them in the shape of a man.

He feels unsatisfied; the case is not resolved. He is considering whether he dares to go for a drink, when his phone pings.

"I started to dig a hole," he reads. *Dig!* he thinks. The killer had not intended the parts to remain above ground. He had readied them for burial. The pathologist is not even sure there is a killer.

He'd lied, told his husband he'd been to the doc, but when he's home alone, he goes into the garden bare-chested, not caring if the neighbours see, and lifts his face to the rain, praying it will wash away the damp hair covering his body. At the same time, he feels a terrible anxiety about the rain ruining the harvest if it continues.

His thoughts drift: the hole, the storm, the seed—

The seed! He'd found it after the storm. Does it have something to do with the man?

He sends the join request to the Facebook group. The moderator sends a stern notice back: it is obligatory to put up a date-stamped profile pic that will be checked for modifications.

It is both a shock and a relief to see the twenty-three who've joined.

After some messaging back and forth, he casually mentions the gold seed. A flood of replies: every single one of them found one too.

The pathologist has no idea where the head is. Or why burying it would be a good idea. But he posts a last message, then arranges to meet the student in the park after his shift.

◊

The rain is still softly falling at 3 a.m. the next morning when the student walks slowly down the stairs, groggy from lack of sleep. She feels a curious sadness for the headless man in her dreams. And a terrible fear. The man is not ordinary. She shuffles down the avenue, too tired to ask any more questions. She does not understand, but somehow understanding is no longer the point.

◊

The pathologist joins the student where she sits on the steps of a monument to an old war. He chain-smokes as he tells her about his parents and the farm, how somehow he had felt the man shiver though him like the wind in the barley, about how he'd invited the group of hairy people to the park, with the promise of a possible cure, but is unsurprised at their absence. He doesn't tell her about his vision.

◊

The student feels like a child listening to a fairy tale. The fields take shape in her imagination. And something more ancient and wild that came before them. When the hairy people emerge from the ring of tangled trees, just before dawn, she can hardly tell if they are real or not.

They stand silently in a circle in the very centre of the park, itself the centre of the city, the pathologist and the student in the middle.

The wind rustles an urgent whisper through the leaves.

"No idea why, but we must dig," says the pathologist, pulling a trowel from his coat.

As the student and pathologist take turns digging, the student hears the one-two, one-two of her speeding heart, beating in sync with the trowel cutting into the earth.

◊

Nothing happens. The pathologist stares morosely into the empty hole. Angry, he takes the seed from his wallet and hurls it in, then sits on the steps of the monument and watches as the hairy people imitate him and throw in their seeds. *Desperate fuckers.* He has just managed to light a cigarette, sheltering it with his coat, when the student yells.

He rushes over, bending into the screaming wind. The trees and bushes thrash wildly in the sudden downpour. Confused by the grass turning to barley around him, by the feverish trill of insects, he looks into the hole.

Darkness. Nothing. His vision in ruins. He holds his hands up to his head, like a man who has lost everything.

The rain stops abruptly as the dawn breaks. He looks again.

Sky blue eyes stare up at him from a severed head with wild, golden hair. Dead. But somehow alive, bright blood spurting from the neck into the soil.

He can't look into the eyes for long.

The trees and bushes flame scarlet, before the soil collapses in over the head and the park is lit with warm golden light.

The pathologist glances down at his hands and sees the hair falling from his fingers. He begins to weep onto smooth cheeks.

◊

After the student tells the pathologist her latest dream about the barleyman, he volunteers to do the paperwork for the eventual disposal of the man's parts. He travels with his previously hairy friends to parks all over the city, carrying small pieces of flesh. They bury the heart last, in the hole where the head appeared.

The student gets an extension and finishes her thesis. She starts a project growing rooftop gardens in the city.

Although the rain stops and the harvest is saved, the pathologist continues to be haunted by the vision of the man's body reunited and whole. It is only in spring, when he notices stubborn shoots pushing everywhere through concrete, that he understands what his vision of wholeness means.

The student notices the shoots too. When she gazes down the avenue, she observes that the florets have turned into lush patches of green. She imagines the patches widening, plants proliferating in parks and streets and on balconies, spreading, connecting, their roots drinking dark, rich blood.

Acknowledgements

Thanks to Christopher Hamilton-Emery at Salt. To Megan Taylor, my sister in arms in our writing endeavours, for her support, wicked sense of humour and brilliant naughtiness. Never a dull moment!

To my wonderful sister, Kerrin, who suffered nobly through my first baby steps in writing, enduring my extremely lengthy phone calls where I went through every query. Luckily for her, my writing improved.

To Nicholas Royle for his inspiring generosity to me and many other writers, his being a stickler for grammar, but most of all for his wacky sense of humour and accomplished cossacking (I know no one else who can do it, to be honest ...).

To the Moniack Mhorers, writing and laughing friends extraordinaire. What would I do without you?

To Cathy Galvin at the Word Factory, for her support and encouragement and get-things-done attitude.

To Leone Ross, my Word Factory Apprenticeship mentor, a writer whose exceptional work I have long admired. She helped me to see even further on stories I considered complete.

Acknowledgements

To the Nottingham Writers' Studio, where I found my first fiction group. And to my fiction groups for all their essential feedback, with special thanks to Roberta Dewa, Megan Taylor, Josie Barrett and Ian Collinson.

Many thanks to the editors of the magazines and anthologies that have published my work, especially to Michael J. DeLuca and Barbara Byar for their excellent editorial suggestions. And extra thanks to Michael J. DeLuca for establishing such a great community of editors at Reckoning Magazine, which I've been so happy to be a part of, and for being so supportive of me and other writers.

Many thanks too to Cleo Gray, Jon McGregor and Tania Hershman, who gave me much-appreciated encouragement.

To my brilliant brother, Dustin, who always cheers me up. To my mother, who steeped me in the cauldron of reading at an early age. To my dad and to Gertrude, departed but never forgotten.

To all my friends, especially Lyns, Sim, Al, Andy, Kay and Sean. And to Duncan, for making me realise you can smash a hole through the wall of your house if you want to, my first lesson in getting started on things.

To everyone I've ever met, to experience, and to our beautiful-ugly world, those bottomless sources of writing inspiration.

Publication Acknowledgements

'The Goldfinch Is Fine' ©2018, originally published in *TSS Publishing*; and *Sunburnt Saints: An Anthology of Climate Fiction* (Seventy2One)

'Mammals, I Think We Are Called' ©2016, originally published in *The Stockholm Review of Literature, Issue 16*

'Everybody Knows That Place' ©2018, originally published in *Black Static, Issue 66* (TTA Press)

'As You Follow' ©2016, originally published in *Flakes of a Fire* (Writing East Midlands Aurora Open Competition 2016); and *Best British Short Stories 2017* (Salt)

'Drowning' © 2019, originally published in *The Shadow Booth, Vol. 4* (edited by Dan Coxon)

'Thin' © 2012, originally published in *Mslexia, Issue 53* (Mslexia Publications Ltd)

Publication Acknowledgements

'Scaffolding' ©2020, originally published in *Mainstream: An Anthology of Stories from the Edges* (Inkandescent)

'I Probably Am a Lonely One' ©2016, originally published in *The Elbow Room Prize 2016* (Elbow Room)

'Wolphinia' ©2016, originally published in *Reckoning Journal, Issue 1* (Reckoning Press); and *Songs for the Elephant Man* (Mantle Lane Press)

'A, and I' ©2022, original to this collection

'Are You Cold, Monkey? Are You Cold?' ©2014, originally published in *Mslexia, Issue 61* (Mslexia Publications Ltd)

'Dividual' ©2018, originally published in *Cōnfingō, Issue 10* (Cōnfingō)

'Grow Your Gorilla' ©2016, originally published in *HISSAC Short Story Competition, 2016* (HISSAC)

'The Edges of Seasons' ©2022, original to this collection

'Pain Is a Liar' ©2021, originally published in *Dreamland: Other Stories* (Black Shuck Books)

'When Death is Over' ©2022, original to this collection

'Hooked' ©2022, original to this collection

'Barleycorn' ©2022, original to this collection

This book has been typeset by
SALT PUBLISHING LIMITED
using Granjon, a font designed by George W. Jones
for the British branch of the Linotype company in the
United Kingdom. It is manufactured using Holmen
Book Cream 70gsm, a Forest Stewardship Council™
certified paper from the Hallsta Paper Mill in Sweden.
It was printed and bound by Clays Limited in Bungay,
Suffolk, Great Britain.

CROMER
GREAT BRITAIN
MMXXII